A WITCH, HER CAT AND THE WHISTLER

A Tale of a Scarborough Witch, her Cat, Smugglers and Spies.

By Graham A. Rhodes

First published 2016
Internet Kindle Edition 2016

Templar Publishing Scarborough N. Yorkshire
Copyright G. A. Rhodes 2016

Conditions of Sale.

This book is sold subject to the condition that it shall not, by way of trade or otherwise, be lent, re-sold, hired out, or otherwise circulated without the publisher's prior consent, in any form of binding or cover other than that in which it is published.

All rights reserved. No part of this publication may be reproduced, stored in a retrieval system, or transmitted, in any form or by any means, electronic, mechanical, photocopying, recording or otherwise, without the prior permission of the publishers and copyright holder.

Also available in the Agnes the Scarborough Witch series –

A Witch, her Cat and a Pirate:
A story of a Scarborough witch, her cat and John Paul Jones

A Witch, her Cat and the Ship Wreckers:
A story of a Scarborough witch, her cat and ship wreckers and highwaymen.

A Witch her Cat and the Devil Dogs:
A story of a Scarborough witch and evil on the North Yorkshire Moors.

A Witch her Cat and A Viking Hoard:
A story of a Scarborough witch and the original Viking settlement of Skathaborg.

Dedication

This is the fifth book of Agnes. As usual, it would have been impossible without the help and encouragement of the following people –
Yvonne, Jesse, Frankie & Heather (& Granddad), Chris, the Badgers of Bohemia, Jo, Tubbs & Missy, Magenta, Anna (whose gig at the SJT started all this off) & all at Cellars and The Merchant, Dennis & Dave, and finally Ysanne in the hope that one day it will turn up in her bookshop.

Many of the streets and places mentioned in this book still exist in Scarborough's old town and up on the moors. They are well worth visiting. Once again I have taken the liberty of using the names of old Scarborough fishing families. I hope they don't mind their ancestors appearing here. However, the names and characters are all fictitious and should not be confused with anyone living or dead.

Character List

Agnes 21st & 18th Centuries
Our hero, an elderly lady who, as far as she knows, is over three hundred years old. She has no memory of who she is or where she came from. She lives in the same cottage in the Old Town of Scarborough in both centuries. She is either a wize woman or a witch, depending on who is telling the story. She is also a computer hacker.

Marmaduke 21st & 18th Centuries
Marmaduke lives with Agnes in her cottage. In the 21st century he is an old, grumpy, one-eared, one-eyed, sardine addicted cat. In the 18th century he is a one eyed, one eared, six-foot high ex-highwayman with very dangerous habits.

Andrew Marks 18th Century
The proprietor of the Chandlery situated on Scarborough's 18th century harbour side. Andrew is the eyes and ears of the small port. Nothing comes or goes in or out the port without him knowing about it, either legal or illegal.

Whitby John 18th Century
Ex-fisherman and landlord of The Three Mariners, Agnes' favourite public house.

Mrs. Whitby John (Nee Pateley) 18th Century
A Captain's widow and the new wife of Whitby John. She is the broom that sweeps the Three Mariners clean.

Salmon Martin 18th Century
A fisherman and regular of the Three Mariners.

Old Sam 18th Century
A storyteller and drinker.

Baccy Lad 18th Century
A young lad eager to please and helper at the Three Mariners.

The Garrison Commander 18th Century
The military commander of the Garrison based at Scarborough's Castle. Posted to Scarborough for a mistake he made during the American War of Independence he is very definitely a soldier of the old school.

Lieutenant Smalls 18th Century
A young military man and the right hand man of the Garrison Commander. An intelligent and thoughtful officer who could go far.

The Whistler 18th Century
A gang leader who haunts the area around Robin Hood's Bay

The Colonel-with-no-name 18th Century
Army intelligence. If you knew more about him he would have to have you killed.

The Sergeant-with-no-name 18th Century
Army intelligence. If you knew more about him he would be the one to arrange your death.

Dancing Jack 18th Century
Ex-highwayman and government agent

Mean Mary 18th Century
Not your average Colonel's daughter and Dancing Jack's right hand woman.

Mrs. Anderson 18th Century
A Robin Hood's Bay landlady.

Jakob 18th Century
Not a rope salesman.

Also featuring numerous smugglers, robbers, thieves, and other ne'er do wells.

A Witch, Her Cat and The Whistler.

Graham A. Rhodes.

Chapter One

It was a hot day in late July and the weather reporter on the television was talking about global warming. There had to be some explanation for the ridiculously hot weather. Agnes fanned herself. She couldn't remember it ever have been so hot and she had a very long memory, one that stretched back long before meteorological records began, and more.

Of course, the weather was creating a summer boom for Scarborough. Now in the twenty-first century as the fishing industry slowly died and the harbour no longer a port, the town was more and more reliant on tourism for its revenue. Down on the foreshore, along the edge of the beach and the harbour tourists walked almost shoulder to shoulder with each other, clutching trays of fish and chips and ice cream cones. Some of the more daring ones even nibbled on hot dogs. Outside the

Newcastle Packet drinkers sat gulping down cold lagers and beers. Cars crawled along the Marine Drive heading for the North Bay, or the South Bay, depending on which way they were facing. The loud music from the Luna Park combined with shouts of the ladies on the shellfish stalls that combined with the music, jangles and jingles from the amusement arcades and screams of the seagulls. All in all Scarborough was living up to its reputation as one of England's most popular holiday resorts.

Agnes fanned herself once more. She was bored. She didn't like the heat. It didn't agree with her. At her age, she thought that shedding an item of clothing was to lose some of her dignity. She even refused to leave her cottage and its yard. Outside was just too crowded. The last time she ventured out she had walked straight into a party of tourists who had stopped outside her cottage to take advantage of a "photo opportunity". As soon as they pointed their cameras at her she shut the door in their face. She looked around her yard looking for her cat. She found the large, ginger haired, one-eyed, one-eared creature hard and fast asleep in the shade of a large bunch of herbs. As she bent down to pick him up she realised he had found the coolest spot in the yard. She hoisted him up under her arm and before he could wake up and do anything about it, she was halfway down her cellar steps and had stepped through the wall.

Agnes's cottage held a great secret. Her cellar held the doorway to another time, not, however, another place. The cellar led Agnes back into eighteenth century Scarborough. To be precise, the late seventeen hundreds, to her own cottage, which had been built in seventeen hundred and twelve. The passing through from one period of time to another never affected Agnes. It did, however, have a large and very fundamental effect on the cat. Now in the cellar, there was no sign of a cat. Instead, there was a large, one-eared, one-eyed ginger haired man complete with a short, pointed beard and whiskers.

He was dressed in a shirt and leather waistcoat, and leggings that were tucked into the tops of a pair of well-worn riding boots. The man adjusted his eye patch and looked quickly behind him to make sure his tail had disappeared. It had but, for a few seconds after every transmutation, it felt like something was still there. Eye patch adjusted, he stroked his whiskers and his pointed ginger beard. His good eye looked at Agnes.

"What?" he asked.

"It's too hot in the twenty-first century, too many tourists. I thought we could take a stroll along the eighteenth-century harbourside. There's no tourists and they haven't invented amusement arcades yet."

Marmaduke gave a shrug. To be honest, despite finding a cool spot in the herbs, he was finding the heat oppressive, and despite his cat habit of sleeping the day away, he too was bored.

Outside the sun shone down on the small cluster of red roofs and narrow cobbled streets. There was plenty of shade as the houses clustered together as if to protect themselves from the cold winters and harsh February gales.

They walked down the Dog and Duck steps and stopped outside the Three Mariners, Agnes' favourite hostelry. The landlady sat outside a polishing cloth in one hand and a large number of spoons, forks, and assorted cutlery were spread out on a cloth at her feet. At her side was a second cloth covered with a pile of bright, shiny cutlery. Agnes smiled. Despite having married Whitby John, the landlord of the Three Mariners over a year ago now, Agnes still had the habit of calling her Mrs. Pateley.

The woman in question was grateful to Agnes from delivering her from a lonely life as a sea captain's widow, and enriching it with the running of a public house complete with an army of cantankerous, but mainly friendly locals, and a husband who doted on her. She liked her new life and was so grateful to Agnes that if she wanted to call her by her old name, well that was fine by her.

Whilst the two women fell to chatting about the weather and then to exchanging gossip Marmaduke walked onto the harbour side, crossing the dirt road packed tight with earth and sand. He wasn't paying attention to anything when he became aware of someone behind him. He walked slowly down the road. Whoever it was followed him. He continued until he came to a narrow alleyway between two wooden buildings.

In the blink of an eye, he ducked into the alley, flashed out an arm and dragged the person by the arm. He swung them around so they were facing him. The surprise on their face was a picture. It then turned to worry as the person realised that the thing poking the bottom of their chin was the tip of a very sharp and pointed dagger. The surprise went two ways. Marmaduke's face turned from a snarl to a look of amazement when he realised he was holding a dagger at the throat of a very determined and very attractive young woman. He took a step back and lowered the dagger. She was tall and wore a frock coat over a pair of riding breeches tucked into a pair of very good riding boots. He noticed that beneath her coat she had a pistol tucked into her belt. He raised an eyebrow. The young woman said nothing but felt her chin where the dagger had been, She looked at her fingers for any sign of blood. There wasn't any.

"Why are you following me?" He asked.

"It's a free country! I was just walking down the road. May I remind you, it was you who assaulted me!" She looked down and brushed some dirt of her jacket.

Marmaduke didn't play games. Anyway, he was never comfortable in the company of women, especially very attractive, young women. He turned and was about to walk out of the alley when he felt a hand tap on his shoulder. He turned.

The punch that landed on the end of his chin made his ears ring and his eyes lose focus. Instantly his hand reached for his pistol. It wasn't there. He shook his head to clear his vision. Then he saw the woman was holding a pistol at his chest. More to the point it was his own pistol. He took a step back and touched the end of his chin. He was sure one of his teeth had become loose.

"That was for dragging me into the alley." She said and lifted the pistol a bit higher. "You are Marmaduke aren't you?" She asked.

Marmaduke could see no point in denying it. He nodded his head.

"Dancing Jack sent me!" she said.

Marmaduke froze. Dancing Jack, ex-highwayman turned Government agent, employed by the army. He smiled as he remembered their time together when Agnes and the two of them rounded up a mercenary army of shipwreckers and highwaymen and uncovered a Dutch plot to disrupt England. He was quickly brought back to the present by the young woman.

"Well?" She asked.

Marmaduke made a sudden move with his hand. The pistol flew up in the air. He spun and caught it. The girl staggered back. Marmaduke looked at the pistol and slide it into his own belt.

"Prove it!" He said.

She fumbled around inside her jacket and pulled out what seemed to be a small coin. She handed it to Marmaduke. He took it carefully making sure the young woman wasn't planning on making any sudden movements. He glanced down at the coin and turned it over. Instantly he recognised it as a token carried by highwaymen to grant them free accommodation and safe passage. It had once belonged to a man called Dammit Johnson, a man unlucky enough to fall foul of Marmaduke and Dancing Jack. He offered the token back to the young woman. She shook her head.

"He said for you to keep it until such time as he can collect it himself."

Marmaduke nodded and carefully placed in his waistcoat pocket.

"What does he want?" asked Marmaduke.

The young woman glanced to her right and to her left. "I'm not sure he would condone my speaking of his affairs in such an open place."

Marmaduke looked up and down the alley. It was

deserted. He shrugged.

"Follow me!" He said and led her out of the alley back onto Foreshore Road.

Once on the road he turned left and retraced his steps back to the Three Mariners. As he led the young woman towards the front door he noticed that Agnes was still engrossed in her conversation. She looked up as he approached and raised an eyebrow.

"A friend?" She asked.

"A messenger!" he replied

Intrigued Agnes ended her conversation and followed Marmaduke and the young woman inside.
Marmaduke chose a table at the far end of the room, well away from the ears of Baccy Lad who followed the progress of the young woman across

the room with eyes wide open. As he stood looking at her and his mouth opened, he became aware of a clicking noise. He turned to see Agnes standing in front of him tapping the bar with her fingernail. "Three tankards of the best!" She said.

As Baccy Lad poured the drinks Agnes looked around the bar. It was very quiet. Most of the customers had taken their drinks outside to enjoy the sunshine. Even Salmon Martin had moved away from his normal spot by the fireplace to sit by the doorway. She walked across to where Marmaduke was seated with the young woman. As she sat down Mary looked at her and turned towards Marmaduke.

"I didn't expect you to bring your mother!" she exclaimed as Agnes made herself comfortable. Marmaduke raised his eyebrows.

"Grandmother!" Agnes said. "Or, maybe Great Grandmother!"

A look of confusion crossed the young woman's face. Marmaduke leant forward.

"Did Dancing Jack ever mention someone called Agnes?" he asked.

The young woman shook her head, Marmaduke sighed. He sensed that Dancing Jack had a very good reason for not mentioning Agnes but for the life of him, he couldn't think of what it could be.

Baccy Lad placed a tray of the three drinks between them. As he turned away Agnes noticed he couldn't keep his eyes off the young woman. She also noticed he was about to walk away without seeing the stool right in front of him. She wondered whether she should say anything. She decided against it. As Baccy Lad tumbled to the floor with a clatter she considered that he had learnt a very important lesson.

The young woman, fully aware of Baccy Lad's

attention, burst out into laughter as the young man lay on the inn's stone flagged floor, trying to disentangle himself from the legs of the upturned stool.

Marmaduke stood up and pulled the young man to his feet. The men at the door turned away and returned to watching the world outside the inn. Baccy Lad brushed himself down and returned behind the bar where, red-faced, he busied himself rearranging the bottles on the shelves behind him. Marmaduke took a sip of his drink as the young woman composed herself.

"Well?" he said eventually.

The young woman returned her attention to him. "I said in private!" She remarked.

Agnes gave a little cough. The young woman turned to look at her.

"I'd better disappear then." Agnes said.

Under the table she twitched her fingers. Then she simply just wasn't there. The young woman's mouth dropped open. With a glint of panic in her eyes, she looked at the stool where Agnes had been seated. Then she looked under the table, then she looked across at Marmaduke.

"It's a neat trick if you can do it!" The voice of Agnes said.

The young woman gave a slight shriek and her face turned white.

"And I can do it!" Agnes said. She was back seated on her stool. The young woman opened her mouth and promptly fainted.

"Dropping like flies over there!" Commented Salmon Martin to the other drinkers standing by the doorway.

Marmaduke lifted the young woman back into her seat. When she came around as first she thought it was raining. Then she realised it was Agnes flicking drops of ale at her face. Annoyed she reached towards the dagger at her belt. That was a big mistake. Two things happened simultaneously. There was a flash of silver and a throwing knife appeared from nowhere pinning her arm to the tabletop. At the same time, a snake shot out of her tankard like a jack-in-a-box. It grew until its face was at the same level as that of the young woman's.

She tried to scream but found that no sound could leave her mouth no matter how hard she tried. She watched transfixed in horror as the snake swayed from side to side, its black, blank eyes staring straight into hers. Then it simply wasn't there. The knife remained in her jacket sleeve, though.

Agnes looked at her "Young lady. First of all Dancing Jack is a friend to both of us. Secondly, his omission of telling you about me is his sense of humour. He knows wherever I go Marmaduke goes. He knows Marmaduke is always at my side. Now either he has had a remarkable loss of memory or, for reasons of his own, he has decided you need a lesson in manners."

The young woman opened her mouth to speak but Agnes lifted her hand.

"Let me introduce myself to you. My name is Agnes, now who are you?" As she spoke she gave the young woman one of her special looks. The young woman didn't stand a chance.

"My name is Mary, I'm a Colonel's daughter. I got recruited a while ago now. I'm working alongside Jack."

As she spoke she wondered why she was revealing information to this elderly woman but found she couldn't stop talking.

"No doubt you are under the command of the Colonel-with-no-name." Agnes remarked.

The young woman's eyes opened wide. "How do you...? He is unknown. He is a secret!"

"Not to us!" Remarked Agnes as she took a deep drink off her ale.

Marmaduke placed his tankard on the table and withdrew his dagger from the young woman's arm and replaced it in the bandoleer inside his jacket.

"Suppose you give me Jack's message now?" He asked.

He looked straight into the young woman's eyes. She tried to hold his gaze, but couldn't. For some reason his eyes reminded her of those of a cat. She nodded and thought for a few seconds to get the wording correct.

"He said to tell you...." She paused trying to remember his exact words.

"Cast your nets towards Saltersgate!" She said finally.

There was silence.

Marmaduke looked at her. "That was it?" he asked.

The young woman nodded. "He didn't have time to say anything else. He was fighting for his life when he bade me to seek you out."

"You mean he's ill? Agnes asked leaning forward.

Mary shook her head. No, he was engaged in sword-play at the time."

Marmaduke leant forward. His face was grim. "You mean you left him to fend for himself?"

The young woman flushed. "He'll be fine. He always is, is Jack!"

She looked at Marmaduke trying to avoid his eyes. "He told me to go. What could I do? He is my senior officer in the field. Do you expect me to disobey a direct order?"

Agnes shook her head. "A bit prickly aren't we?"

Mary flared her nostrils and turned to her. "Of course I'm prickly. He needed my help in that fight. Instead, he orders me to go and then takes them on all by himself. The idiot!"

She said the last words with such passion that Agnes began to suspect there was more to Mary and Jacks relationship than she had cared to mention.

Agnes got up and walked across to the bar where she spoke to Baccy Lad, then as he disappeared into the back for a moment she returned to the table and sat down. A moment later Baccy Lad reappeared carrying a bowl of water. He carefully placed it on the table in front of Agnes and even more carefully made his way back to the bar.

Agnes reached into her pocket and pulled out some herbs and spices that she sprinkled over the surface of the water. She looked up at Marmaduke.

"May I borrow the token?"

A question rose at the back of Mary's mind. How did the woman know about the token? She was about to say something when she caught the look on Marmaduke's face. He slightly shook his head at her as he reached out across the table and handed Agnes the small round token. She shut up and watched as Agnes held the token in one hand and passed her other hand over the top of the bowl. Then she gave a little gasp as a face appeared in the water. It was the face of Dancing Jack. She panicked when she saw his eyes were shut. The panic gave way to annoyance when the image in front of her expanded. Now she could see that Jack was asleep in a rather large and very grand four poster bed. When she saw a woman seated on the bed next to her she slapped the table so hard that the bowl lifted an inch into the air. Agnes pulled her head back quickly to avoid getting wet. She looked across to Mary.

"Let's not jump to any conclusions!" She said, and bent down over the bowl once again.

This time the vision revealed the woman to be bathing Jacks forehead with a damp cloth. Every so often she would bend over and rinse it out. Mary's anger turned to concern.

"He's wounded! I knew I shouldn't have left him."

Agnes looked across the table at her. "It was sensible. He wouldn't have concentrated if you were fighting at his side. Perhaps you would have both been killed. At least he survived and the message got through. Whichever way you look at things I would say you got a good result."

Mary was about to say something and then thought better of it. The elderly woman had a point.

"Where is he?" Asked Marmaduke.

"In some woman's boudoir!" Exclaimed Mary.

Marmaduke shook his head. "Geographically!"

Mary reddened. "We were in Kingston upon Hull."

Marmaduke nodded. "And what were you doing in Hull?"

Mary lifted her tankard to her lips and took a swig. She then replaced the tankard on the table and looked up at Marmaduke.

"I'm not sure I'm allowed to tell you that information!"

Agnes looked at her. "Is that because it's a secret or because you don't actually know?"

Mary reddened again. "As far as I know he was asked to keep an eye out for a gang of smugglers. He was watching the ships coming in and out of the port."

"Any idea what he was looking for?"

"He said it was better I didn't know, "What you don't know won't hurt you", he said. I did notice he became very attentive when any ship landed from the Continent though."

Agnes flexed her fingers. "Perhaps he's on the lookout for the Dutch." She said.

Marmaduke raised an eyebrow again. They had experienced the Dutch influence the year previously when they unravelled a plot to arm private militias in the countryside. The fact that England was currently at war with the Dutch had completely passed him by.

"From what I can make out we declared war on the Dutch last December. Something to do with them supporting the American Colonists by shipping supplies to them. No one's taken it very seriously though as the Dutch Government are a bit unsettled at the moment. I don't know much more. Though, I know a man who probably does."

Mary blinked at Agnes as she wondered how she knew about the current political situation. Her thoughts were interrupted by Marmaduke.

"What's that got to do with Saltersgate?" He asked.

Mary drained her tankard. "What's Saltersgate?" she asked.

Marmaduke smiled. "It's an inn that sits astride the main moorland route to Whitby. It's a place to avoid. A haunt of cut throats and smugglers. It's where most of the contraband landed along the coast passes through on its way inland. Even the army hesitate to go near the place. People tend to go in there and never come out!"

Mary shook her head. "I had no idea. I've never heard of the place before he gave me that message."

Agnes tutted. "Secrets! Can't do with them!"

Her comment almost caused Marmaduke to choke on his drink. Of all the people he had ever met Agnes held more secrets than all of them put together.

Agnes placed her tankard on the table. "Come on. Let's go see Andrew. If anyone can tell us what's going on with the Dutch he can. Before we get involved in anything I do like to know what's going on! Anyway what else can we do?"

She looked across at Marmaduke "Unless you fancy a trip to Saltersgate?"

Marmaduke shook his head. A trip to the inn would take a lot of planning and even more preparations. Saltersgate wasn't a place to treat lightly.

Agnes led them out of the Mariners and along the Foreshore until they arrived at the chandlery owned by Andrew Marks. As they approached Agnes spotted him standing by the front door. He was checking a sheaf of papers and every so often looked up at the ships moored in the harbour. When he saw who was approaching he quickly folded the paper up and placed it into his inside jacket pocket. The action didn't escape Agnes's attention. She chose to ignore it. What she didn't know she wouldn't have to do something about it.

She flashed Andrew a smile.

"Andrew we've come to pick your brains!"

Inwardly Andrew gave a groan. He had been involved with Agnes and her unusual adventures before. They were always complicated and always involved a lot of strange occurrences. Sometimes they even involved death. Without saying a word he ushered them through his shop and into his private office. Once inside he realised that the heat of the day had made the room too warm. He turned and opened a window When he turned back he noticed that Agnes had sat in his best office chair. He gave another little inward sigh. It was turning into one of those days.

At first everything went fine. Agnes quizzed him about the political situation with the Dutch. That bit was easy. Andrew explained that the outbreak of war at the end of the previous year had proved a mixed blessing for him. Bad because shipments of timber from the Nordic countries had virtually ceased, and now, seven months on, the port was beginning to feel the loss of the trade. Good because shipments of illicit goods had trebled. The excisemen were overstretched, as were both the Army and Navy. The war on the American continent was occupying every available soldier and most of the Navy. Now the Navy was fighting a war on two fronts. Along the American East Coast and out in the North Sea where they were attempting to blockade Dutch and Continental ports. Agnes had to admit that Andrew knew his business. Then she dropped her little bombshell.

"What do you know of Saltersgate?"

The colour drained from Andrews' face.

"Don't even think of going there!" He exclaimed.

Mary gave a little snort. "It can't be that bad surely!"

Andrew gave her a long hard stare. "Yes it can, and more. They'll cut your throat and stand by taking bets on how long it will take for you to die. Think of the most violent and bloody thirsty bunch of thieves and brigands you've ever come across and then double, no treble it. Going in there would be to enter the seventh circle of hell. Leave the place well alone. The Army and the Excise do!"

He paused and then a penny dropped at the back of his mind. "Hang on. Why mention the Dutch and Saltersgate in the same conversation? Don't even think of telling me they are linked somehow. Whatever it is, count me out!"

He looked at Agnes. "Agnes, with you I've been places and seen things that no normal man could have dreamt of. Please take my advice, don't get involved with Saltersgate. They are not normal up there. They're a tribe, they're so close they are impossible to infiltrate. Everyone up there is someone's brother, or cousin, or some relation,

Strangers tend to be killed on sight, and nobody asks any questions, before or after."

Agnes nodded. "I'll tell you the full story, at least, as much of it as we know."

She then told him of Dancing Jack and his mission. When it came to the introduction of Mary Andrew looked across at the young woman.

"The army employs you?" He asked rather ungallantly.

Mary immediately took umbrage. "And why not? I'll have you know a woman can get places a man can never go. There are other ways to get information than at the tip of a sword!"

Both Andrew and Marmaduke remained silent. Agnes could see their imaginations working overtime. She smiled. She rather liked Mary. At least she had guts. It would be interesting to work alongside another woman. Anyway, she trusted Dancing Jack's judgment. There was a reason he trusted her to be at his side. He knew what he was doing.

Agnes gave a slight cough. "And that Andrew is why we are here. Somehow there is a connection between the Dutch and Saltersgate. We need to find out what and as you have eyes and ears all over the harbour you're the man best positioned to know what's coming and going."

Andrew scratched his head and thought to himself. "There's not a lot happening at the moment. Oh, there's a steady trade coming and going, most of it slipping under the excisemen's noses, but nothing to raise any suspicions."

He paused and then added. "Mind you I can only speak for Scarborough. There could be all sorts going on in Whitby, or Robin Hood's Bay. I mean you know how tight-lipped they are up there. More illicit trade goes through the Bay than anywhere else, and it has a direct route across the moors to Saltersgate."

Agnes thought about it. He was right. If something untoward was going on Robin Hood's Bay would be the place. The people there were as close as those in Saltersgate. Andrew was still talking.

"Of course it's a long coast. If Jack was looking at Hull, well it could be that the answer is further down the coast. There's plenty of places to land illicit cargo between here and there,"

Marmaduke looked across to Mary. "Who was Jack fighting?" he asked.

Mary shuffled in her seat and looked around her anxiously. Agnes realised her predicament.

"You're worried about military secrets?" She asked.

Mary slowly nodded. "The Colonel-with-no-name is beyond military secrets. He impressed both me and Jack that we were dealing with the safety of the realm. State secrets!"

Andrew let out a little snort. "If you mean the English fleet led by Hyde Parker, everyone knows about that!"

"I don't!" Said Agnes.

Andrew turned to her. "For the last couple of months, Parker has had a fleet out there blocking Dutch ports and harrying the continental shipping. From what I have gathered it's being supplied from Hull."

Mary turned to him with a look of shock on her face. "No one is meant to know about that!"

Andrew laughed. "Come on girl, It's a fleet! Even the good Colonel can't hide an entire fleet. It's been seen by dozens of ships and their men. When the men arrive in harbour they talk, then they get drunk, and then they talk some more. If you ever want to find out what's happening out there..." he nodded towards the window out of which they could see the harbour and beyond that the North Sea. "...all you have to do is buy a drink in The Beehive, The Dolphin, The Three Mariners, The...."

Mary cut him off. "I get the idea!"

Agnes looked across at her. "Just how long have you worked for the Colonel?"

Mary shuffled in her seat. "A couple of months!"

Agnes smiled. "It was Jack that recruited you wasn't it?"

Mary nodded.

Agnes continued. "Why don't you tell us your story. You're among friends, and it will help us. Now as far as I remember you told us you were a Colonel's daughter."

Mary paused and looked around at the people sat in the chandlery office. It was evident to her that she was among people Jack trusted.

"My father was in charge of a unit called The Hessians."

Marmaduke raised his head. Andrew noticed and interrupted Mary's story.

"The Hessians, German mercenaries. Seems that King George hasn't enough troops of his own so his Government hired them and promptly sent them off to the Americas."

Mary cut back in. "Well, my father was one of their Colonels." She lowered her voice. "He was killed at somewhere called Trenton."

Andrew let out a low whistle. "Hells teeth! That's where Washington crossed the Delaware. He captured the entire Trenton garrison!"

Mary nodded. "Only he didn't capture my father. He was killed leading an escape across something called Assunpink Creek."

Agnes tapped the desktop. "That was five or six years ago now." She nodded towards Andrew.

"We've had our history lesson. Let her tell her story."

Andrew looked slightly offended until Agnes flashed him one of her smiles and then turned back to Mary.

"What happened next?"

"After he died my mother tried to keep the household going but father had debts. She did her best to honour them but two years after he died she fell ill. She died before the month was out. I was sent to an aunt. She did her best to marry me off to a succession of old men. I ran away."

Agnes looked at her. "You took to the road?"

Mary shook her head. "Not at first. At first I sought work. I ended up working in a tavern. One day Jack arrived. He paid me to keep an eye open for him."

Marmaduke raised an eyebrow. He knew all about the people who worked in taverns. Most of them were in the pay of footpads and highwaymen, pointing them in the direction of travellers who were suitable targets for robberies and hold ups. Mary saw his expression and felt she was being judged. She looked into his eyes, then she looked away again. They were disconcerting, they looked too much like the eyes of a cat. She continued talking.

"It wasn't unusual. A lot of the ostlers and taproom keepers did the same. The inn was on a major route out of London, there were rich pickings to be had. That was when I realised Jack wasn't like the others who sought out information. Oh, he looked and acted like a regular highwayman, only with a bit more swagger, but he wasn't interested in the typical traveller. After a while I began to wonder if he really was a highwayman after all, until the night of the fire"

Everyone suddenly lifted their heads towards the young woman but no one spoke so she continued.

"One night there was a party of gentlemen staying overnight. Jack arrived shortly after. As they dined I let him gain access to their rooms. He slipped up. Unknown to me they had left one of their number in the room upstairs. There was a fight. The first I knew something was wrong was when Jack came crashing downstairs, followed by a man with a sword. As soon as his friends saw what was happening they leapt to their friend's assistance. Jack was backed into a corner. I grabbed a bottle from behind the bar and smashed it over one of their heads. He went down and the others turned. It gave Jack the chance he needed. He leapt onto the bar. They followed slashing and hacking at him. Bottles and glasses went flying in all directions. The rest of the customers made for the door. Then one of the men drew a pistol. Jack made to leap out of the way and knocked over a candelabra. The flames took hold and before anyone realised it the bar was on fire. The flames must have found some spilled brandy. As the fire spread the men continued fighting, again I came to Jacks assistance."

She paused and her eyes seemed to drift back to the day.

"I've no idea where it came from, but I found myself with a dagger in my hand. One of the men raised his sword to make a killing stroke. Before he could bring it down I stabbed him under his raised arm. The next thing I remember is Jack dragging me through the door and towards the stables. We found two horses and, as we rode away the entire inn was engulfed in flames. I heard later that the place burned to the ground."
She stopped talking and the room fell silent.

Eventually Agnes spoke. "Who were the men Jack fought?"

Mary shook her head. "To this day I've no idea who they were. I do know they seemed to be foreign, but I've no idea what. I've no idea if they even escaped the fire."

"Security of the realm!" Remarked Andrew.

Mary nodded. "That's what Jack said. Since that

night I've travelled with him. I was his eyes and ears. I would get work in a tavern and let him know what was going on."

She looked across at Andrew and smiled. "That's what I meant by a woman being able to go where men cannot. If you keep your eyes and ears open its surprising what information you can gather serving drinks."

As Andrew's cheeks took on a slight pinkish glow Agnes chuckled aloud.

Marmaduke tried his best not to smile. "But yet you've only been working for the Colonel for a couple of months."

Mary nodded. "Jack would always say the time wasn't right, then one day he said it was. He said he was better the Government paid me rather than it coming out of his own pockets. He took me to London where I met the Colonel and was put on the official payroll. Two days later we were sent to Hull. Then Jack got attacked and here I am."

Marmaduke looked at her. "You still haven't mentioned who the attackers were."

Mary shut her eyes and continued. "There were four of them. Foreign. They just arrived in Hull from a ship carrying Swedish colours, but they weren't Swedes, I think they might have been French. Anyway, they discovered Jack was taking an interest in them. I was covering his back when one of them grabbed me from behind. The fight was fierce. He managed to free me and told me to run. His actual words were, find Marmaduke in Scarborough, tell him to cast his net towards...."

"Saltersgate!" Marmaduke finished the sentence for her.

Andrew sighed. "Hell's teeth. Dutch, French and even worse Saltersgate! What in the name of all that's holy has Jack got himself involved in."

"More to the point," replied Marmaduke, "What's he got us involved in?"

Agnes remained silent. She was thinking. The noise from the harbour drifted into the room from the open window. Outside the people of the harbour were going about their regular business. Fishwives gutted and thrust the filleted herrings into barrels ready for salting. Sailors arrived in port and made their way to the nearest harbourside taverns, staggering from tavern to tavern. She brought her attention back inside the room. She was a bit surprised to find that everyone was looking at her. She gave a slight shrug of her shoulders.

"I suppose we had better start at Robin Hood's Bay!"

Andrew shook his head. "Are you being serious?"

Agnes looked back at him. "Perfectly. What better place to start? We know that everything that passes through the Bay ends up in Saltersgate."

"I'm not too sure I'll be made welcome in the Bay!" Marmaduke said.

He looked across to Mary. "Jack and I had a bit of a set to up there. They might remember me!"

Agnes smiled. "Well my girl, time to put into practice what you've preached."

Everyone looked puzzled. Agnes looked around them all. "Let's find out if woman really can illicit information where men can't!"

Chapter Two

The following morning the post chase from Scarborough stopped at the top of the small town of Robin Hood's Bay. The driver climbed down and opened the carriage door. Out stepped an elderly lady and her young companion. The Elderly woman was dressed in a fine, white bonnet and a long flowing, slightly out of fashion dress with a shawl wrapped around her shoulders. As she disembarked the driver lifted a small trunk from the back of the coach. He looked around and signalled to a young man who was standing against the wall of a large house. The young man stepped forward.

"Two ladies seeking lodgings!" he said.

The young boy nodded. "Mrs. Anderson down the Bay has rooms available."

The elderly lady looked at the young man. "Are they clean? I won't stay anywhere if it's not clean!"

The young man nodded.

"And no inns!" the lady continued. "Drink is an abomination. I won't stay anywhere were strong drink is purveyed!"

The young man continued nodding "It's not an inn. Mrs. Anderson runs a boarding house. You can eat your dinner from her floors, and you get a sea view."

"Young man, eating from the floor is not a good recommendation. However, a sea view sounds most attractive." The elderly woman said before nodding her consent.

It took the young man a short while to load the trunk onto the back of a donkey. Once secured, he led the donkey and the two women down the long, steep and twisted road from the top of the hill down through the town to the seafront where the sea lapped onto a cobbled slipway.

As they walked behind him, the two women linked arms. To all appearances they seemed like an elderly spinster aunt and her young niece. It was just the illusion Agnes wanted to achieve.

As they sauntered down the hill the two woman looked to their left and right at the number of small ginnels and alleyways that branched off the main road, leading to other houses and small hidden yards. The town seemed to be a hotch-potch of small houses clinging onto the steep slope. On the main street were a number of shops. Mary smiled as Agnes stopped in front of dressmakers and began to sing the praises of a dress displayed in the shop window. She waited just long enough to attract the dressmaker's attention, but as he opened the door to greet her, she walked away fanning

herself with a rather elaborate paper fan that Mary had never seen before. As she wondered where it had come from Agnes repeated the process in front of a greengrocer's shop, a shop selling hardware, a confectioners and a shop that sold medicines and perfumes. Mary smiled. By the time they had reached the bottom end of the hill every shopkeeper in town knew of the arrival of a wealthy woman and her young companion. As Mary knew full well, shopkeepers talk.
They arrived at their lodgings and Mrs. Anderson showed them to her to best rooms. Agnes made a great point of running her finger over the mantelshelf and windowledges inspecting for dust. There wasn't any. They took the rooms.

The next hour was spent in unpacking the trunk, hanging dresses up, placing things in drawers and looking through the window, down the street to where they could see the advancing tide dashing its waves onto the slipway. Once everything had been put away the two ladies decided to take a constitutional around the streets at the bottom of the town.

The walk took them passed The Laurel Inn and down to a grocery shop and a large building called the Bay Hotel that stood on the very edge of the slipway itself. As they walked along Mary wondered how the houses hung onto the cliffs without tumbling into the sea beneath them.
The little square at the head of the slipway housed a shop and a group of small sheds where fishing nets hung out to dry, waiting to be mended. Small boats had been dragged onto the cobbles, out of the reach of the rising tide. The two ladies were not by themselves. Gentlemen strolled up and down the hill. Tradesmen scurried between the houses. Fishwives walked briskly in and out of the alleys between the houses. Fishermen gathered around their nets talking whilst mending, their large needles flashing in the sunlight. By the doorway of the Dolphin Inn Agnes noticed a group of men. There was something about the way they stood.

She nudged Mary. As Mary turned to look at them she felt the hair on the back of her neck bristle. Smugglers and footpads, she recognised them immediately after all, she had spent the last few years in their company.

When they returned to their accommodation Mary joined Agnes in her room. Agnes had removed her shoes and was massaging her feet.

"How anyone can walk in these shoes is a mystery!" she said without looking up.

Mary was about to say something when Agnes held her finger to her lips. Mary watched as Agnes then waved a hand in the air and moved her fingers. At first the younger woman thought the older one was suffering from cramp. Agnes soon put her right.

"A spell!" She said, "We can't be overheard now. Mrs. Anderson might be up to date with her dusting but she's a member of this community. We trust no one, understand?"

Mary nodded. She began to realise the elderly lady wasn't what she seemed. This was getting more interesting by the minute. She became aware of Agnes looking at her.

"So what are your impressions of Robin Hood's Bay?"

Mary thought. "A nice little place. Perfect for smugglers!"

Agnes nodded. "It was only a couple of years ago that a pitched battle between smugglers and excisemen happened just out there." She nodded towards the window.

"There was a fall out over two hundred kegs of gin and brandy. The streets are so narrow with secret passages and doors between the houses that a keg of brandy can be moved from the beach to the top of the town without leaving any of the houses!"

She looked back at Mary. "Did you happen to notice that a lot of the women seemed pregnant?"

Mary thought about it. "I didn't really notice." Agnes nodded. "Far too many for a place this size. I would hazard a guess that they are carrying contraband under their skirts. Moving it around from house to house."

She paused and thought for a few seconds before continuing. "Mind you, I know for a fact that smuggling has been going in these parts for decades, probably centuries. The Colonel-with-no-name wouldn't be after smugglers. That's not, how did you put it? "A question of security of the Realm."

Mary reddened slightly when her words were

spoken back to her. They did seem a bit pompous. She listened as Agnes continued with her thoughts.

"The man is looking for something else, something out of the ordinary. Maybe it's something to do with the Dutch, whether it's something else, I don't know. We need to take a closer look."

With that, she reached into a pocket that wasn't on the dress and pulled from it a small silver salver. She reached across to the dressing table and took a pitcher of water from its matching bowl. She poured some of the water into the silver salver and placed it carefully on the small bedside table.

"Let's have a closer look!" she said.

Mary watched as Agnes took a pinch of herbs and spices out from the invisible pocket and sprinkled them over the water. The elderly lady then passed her hands over the surface and an image appeared. It was of the slipway outside. Mary could see some men pulling a boat off the beach onto the cobbled stonework. She could see the stream as it emerged from a culvert that ran between and under houses to reappear as a stream that ran down the steep hill parallel with the main road.

The vision shifted and followed the smaller of the two streets leading back up the hill. It paused outside a small inn.

Agnes glanced up at Mary. "That's the reason Marmaduke doesn't want to be seen here. He and Jack had a bit of an altercation in there. He thinks he might be remembered. They have long memories around here."

"Once seen never forgotten!" Mary said.

Agnes gave her one of those looks. "Which one, Jack or Marmaduke."

Mary flushed slightly. "Both of them actually!"

Agnes smiled and Mary turned away.

Agnes watched the comings and goings around the tavern for a few minutes. Nothing seemed out of place. She moved her hand and the image moved up the street. She paused to watch a man trying in vain to lead his donkey higher up the street. For some reason the donkey refused to move and, to make its point, had placed it's behind firmly on the cobbled road. No matter what the man did, the animal simply refused to move. A few people had gathered around offering advice, one fisherman even going as far as to aim a kick at the donkey's rear end. It had the desired effect. The donkey rose to its four feet. What happened next wasn't desired, especially by the fisherman. The donkey seemed to pause and then place its weight on its front legs before leaning forward and lashing out with its rear legs. The kick caught the fisherman full in the chest. He fell backwards onto the hard cobbles and lay there with his hands clutching his chest. People ran up to him. One of them tried lifting his head. The injured man tried to get up and, with a bit of help from the people around him, managed to stand on his feet,

"Nothing broken!" Remarked Agnes, "Just a broken rib and a bit of bruising."

Mary didn't answer and Agnes glanced sideways. The young woman was looking out of the window, standing to one side, behind a large damask curtain. Agnes looked back into the bowl.

The donkey was now rearing up and one of the wicker panniers it carried slipped its rope. The donkey, looking for someone else to kick spun around, and the pannier overturned spilling its load.

As she watched the scene Agnes noticed that instead of salted fish the pannier seemed to be filled with small packets covered in a thick waterproof, waxy paper, each the size of a brick.

When the man realised his load had come adrift he let go of the donkey, grabbed the packets and quickly stuffed them back into the pannier. Few people had noticed as most of them were keeping their eyes on the donkey and its antics, making sure they were nowhere within kicking range. Others were paying attention to the injured man who was standing at the side of the road, holding onto a wall and accepting a drink from a well-wisher who had offered him a small flagon. He still winced as his free hand examined the area around his chest. Agnes looked on as the man leading the now more willing donkey continued on their way up the hill.

Agnes wondered to herself about the packages in the pannier. It was obvious the man was carrying some sort of contraband. Whatever was in the packages they must surely have travelled by sea, otherwise why the waxed and waterproof packaging? Too small for gin and brandy. The wrong shape for tobacco, too small for salt and silk. She was still wondering when Mary spoke from by the window.

"We are being watched!" She said quietly.

Agnes continued looking into her scrying bowl. "How do you know it's us that's being watched?" Mary remained by the window. "Well, whoever he is he's keeping an eye on this building."

"Perhaps he's watching someone else. Keep looking." Agnes replied as she moved her hand over the water.

The image blurred and then reappeared this time showing an aerial view of the houses and small streets. She reached into her pocket and added a pinch of powder. The image shifted slightly. It now appeared as if someone had removed the roofs of the houses. Now Agnes could see inside every house. She repeated the motion and it seemed as if the fabric of the houses had simply dissolved leaving only a network of alleyways, tunnels and hidden passages leading from the stream at the bottom of the hill to the top of the village, where it reappeared in a large shed. Along its course there were a number of offshoots and dead ends. As she examined the routes of the tunnels Agnes wondered at the hours of work and imagination that had gone into their construction. She realised that many of the tunnels led to the cellars of public houses and taverns whilst others led to the cellars of houses. It was a complex network and she came to the opinion that anyone entering them without a full knowledge of the way it worked would soon become disoriented and lost. She stared at the network and blinked. Now it was fixed in her head. As she often said, a little knowledge might prove very useful.

She moved her hand and the image of the tunnels dissolved. Once again she was looking down on the chimneys red tiled roofs. She looked down on the small streets wondering if she could find the man leading the donkey. There was no sign of him. She found herself wondering about his packages and their contents. She became aware that Mary was speaking once again. She looked at the young woman.

"I was saying that someone has just left our lodgings and the man outside has followed him."

Agnes walked across the room and looked out of the window. Across the small square and at the far end of the slipway she saw the shape of a man disappear around the corner of a building and head up the road. She looked back at the slipway. Sure enough, a man dressed in rough and weathered clothing was also watching. As the first man turned the corner the second man followed him.

Agnes turned to Mary. "I wonder what that's all about?"

Mary shook her head. "The man who left our

lodgings was rather well dressed. He didn't look like he came from around here."

Agnes looked at her with a raised eyebrow. "He could be the local doctor or..."

Mary cut her off with a shake of her head. "No, I don't know why, but he's not local. I've spent the last few years watching travellers I can tell. Anyway, why would a local be staying here?"

Agnes clicked her tongue. "He could be paying a visit."

"I'm going to find out!" Mary suddenly said.

She turned and with a swish of her skirts she left the room and went downstairs. Agnes gave a slight shrug and went back to her scrying bowl. She moved her hand and the image of a man appeared. He was walking up the street near to where the donkey had recently misbehaved. She looked closely at him. The first thing she noticed was that he seemed to be walking casually, occasionally looking to his right and his left. The second thing she noticed was that Mary was right. The man was very well dressed. She doubted if such a coat could be purchased this side of York. The man looked like he knew where he was going. He confirmed that when he suddenly made a sharp right turn into a small alleyway. Halfway down he stopped and rapped on a side door. After a few seconds the door opened. It looked like a few words were exchanged and the man entered. Agnes looked down the alley. Sure enough, the man following him had stopped at the end. He leant casually on the side of the building on the main street.

Nothing happened for a number of minutes apart from the man at the end of the alley taking a small white pipe out from his jacket and begin to slowly fill it.

"I bet there was no duty paid on that!" Agnes said

to herself.

As he lit the pipe Agnes noticed that the man's eyes never left the doorway in the alley. Time passed. Then the door must have opened quickly as the first man suddenly appeared in the alley and walked briskly towards the street. As he set off the man at the end of the alley straightened up, placed his pipe in his pocket and set off down the alley. When they were a couple of steps away from each other the gentleman glanced up. He was too late. There was a blur of movement and before Agnes could do anything about it, the man had sunk to his knees and then tumbled face forwards, blood gushing from a large cut that had appeared across his throat. As he lay there his attacker quickly knelt at his side and began rifling through the dying man's pockets. He found what he was looking for and stuffing it in his own pocket quickly progressed down the alleyway. As he passed the doorway the dead man had just left he stopped and whistled. It was just a few notes that marked the beginning of a tune. Then he took to his heels and was soon lost in the maze of small passages, alleyways, and backyards. Agnes blinked, startled by what she had just witnessed. She jumped slightly as Mary re-entered the room.

"The landlady said he is a foreign gentleman, here to negotiate the sale of rope and twine. She says he's a regular visitor, he comes here twice or three times a year."

"Well he won't be selling any more rope!" Agnes exclaimed.

Mary tilted her head in the form of an unspoken question. Agnes continued.

"He's dead. He had his throat cut a few minutes ago."

Mary looked shocked. "How do you know?"

Agnes nodded towards the scrying bowl. "I watched it happen!"

Mary gave a little shudder. "Was it done by the man I saw watching the house?"

Agnes nodded. "I think so. Whoever he was he was quick. The man was a killer. I doubt many locals could make such a killing blow so quickly. Whoever our foreign gentlemen was someone wanted him dead, but only after he had completed his visit!"

She held up her hand. "Perhaps he was completing some sort of transaction. Then when the transactions completed he's killed and robbed."

Mary nodded. "It makes sense!"

Agnes turned and looked out of the window. "Of course the killer was in cahoots with whoever the unfortunate man was dealing with. Otherwise why did he stop at the door and give a signal?"

Mary looked at Agnes "He whistled?"

Agnes nodded. Then she pursued her lips and whistled the first few notes of the tune.

"Just like that!" she said.

Mary looked puzzled. "How did you know the tune? I mean, that bowl of yours. You see the pictures but you can't hear anything."

Agnes smiled "I read lips!"

Mary had to think about that for a minute. Then she realised she'd better stop thinking about it and let it pass. The woman probably could lip read. Anyway, there was a murder to think about!

"It must have been a signal that the deed was

done."

Agnes nodded. "That was the signal to them inside that the deed was done, for them not to come out. It told them there was a body in the alley and the less they know about it the better. If they came out and stumbled over it they would have to report it. They'll stay inside until someone has found it and it's been dealt with. That way there are no awkward questions."

Mary looked at Agnes in a new light. "Did the Colonel-with-no-name ever try to recruit you?" She asked.

Agnes smiled. "I would have turned him down. I have my duty. However, it is not to the Crown, nor the Government. My duty is to the people of the Old Town, and believe me young lady, I have my work cut out looking after that lot."

She paused and looked directly at Mary. "Anyway,

it seems that I am working for him, indirectly. Jack has asked for help, he's a friend. Around here we help our friends."

Mary reddened slightly. Agnes noticed and smiled at her. "Sorry. I didn't intend any slight. Goodness knows, without the likes of Jack and the Colonel-with-no-name, the country would be in an even bigger mess."

She brushed down the front of her dress. "Speaking of mess, let's see what we can discover. Get your bonnet. It's time that two ladies took their constitutional."

They left the lodgings and played at being tourists, slowly following the footsteps of the assassin and his victim. As they walked up the street Agnes nudged her companion and nodded further up the street. A small crowd had begun to gather at the head of a small alley.

"Looks like they've found the body!" She whispered.

As they drifted forward towards the people a constable walked towards them.

"Better not come too close ladies. There has been an unfortunate accident. Far too upsetting for ladies like yourselves. I suggest you return to the bottom of the street and take the other road. Anyway, the shops are much better up there."

With that, he turned and walked back to the head of the ally. The small crowd parted as he passed through them

"Pompous, self-important, condescending prig!" Mary exclaimed.

Agnes smiled. "You're forgetting we're ladies. We are supposed to be delicate creatures, protected and shielded from the wickedness of the world. As long as we are dressed like this we'll be talked down to, condescended at, and generally pushed into the background."

Mary was about to say something but Agnes raised her hand. "Don't! I know what you are about to say, is not right and it's not fair, but it's going to be like that for the next three hundred years! Now watch and learn."

With that she turned back and looked to where the Constable was standing, ordering the small crowd to stand clear. Agnes moved her fingers.

Suddenly the Constable jumped and clapped his hand onto the back of his neck. They could hear his expletives echo down the street. Agnes rose to her full height and shouted up the road.

"Sir! Your immodest language is far more upsetting than anything you wish to shield us from!"

She then turned quickly on her heel and, taking Mary's arm, walked back down the hill towards the slipway.

Mary looked at her.

"Bee sting!" replied Agnes.

Mary laughed. Agnes smiled. Now she could see why Jack had taken a shine to her.

They turned the corner and proceeded up the second road passing the shops and houses they had walked passed earlier. As they passed the dressmakers Agnes stopped and looked in the window where a dress was displayed on a wooden mannequin.

"I can't understand what people see in shopping." She said.

Mary sighed. "Just the type of dress a General's

daughter would wear. It seems like a lifetime ago!"

Agnes linked her arm through Mary's and the pair walked on up the street. Eventually they came to a small tea shop and Agnes led them through the door and to two seats at a table near to the window.

It was delicious, served in small porcelain cups with matching saucers. It was accompanied by a three tiered dish holding a number of decorative dainties and small cakes. They ate and drank as ladylike as they could. They laughed as they competed to see who could hold out their cup with the most outstretched little finger. Agnes had just popped her third dainty into her mouth when Mary nodded towards the street.

"What do you think that's all about?"

Agnes looked to see a group of men dressed in long coats, hats pulled down over their heads shielding the upper part of their faces. They were walking down the hill with their swords drawn. She also noticed that at least two of them held pistols. They looked like they were on some very serious business.

"Smugglers?" Mary asked.

Agnes continued looking out of the window.

"Possibly, or possibly friends of the dead man come to seek revenge?"

Mary nodded. "Shall we follow them?"

Agnes turned back to the table and looked at the remains of the afternoon tea. Only one dainty remained on the plate. She picked it up and popped it into her mouth.

"Might as well!" She said.

They left the teashop pausing only to wince at the

size of the bill as Agnes paid for her indulgence. As she checked her change she noticed a small coin among the usual pence. She said nothing but slipped it into her pocket. She would examine that later.

They followed the men downhill until they reached the slipway once again. They looked across to their lodgings. Three of the men they were following were standing outside the door whilst a fourth was in a heated discussion with the landlady. As soon as she saw the two ladies appear she said something. The man turned to look at them.

Agnes decided that the constitutional was over and walked up to the door with Mary following. One of the men she passed made a comment and Agnes turned and fixed him with a hard look. He just stared back. She altered her look and slightly raised an eyebrow. The man took a step backwards and reddened. Mary took a step towards him

"I believe you just passed comment about my appearance sir, Please do not keep it to yourself!"

The landlady quickly stepped between them.

"I apologise Miss. I'm sure the gentleman did not intend any slight. Please accept my assurance it will not happen again. The gentlemen were just leaving."

With that, she turned and opened the door for them. Silently the pair walked into the house and walked across the small hall and ascended the stairs to their room. As they reached the first-floor landing they could hear a noisy whisper and then the door closing.

Once they were inside their room Agnes waved her arms and made a few movements with her hands.

"Right, now we can't be overheard." She said as she sat in the large easy chair by the window.

Mary sat on the bed and kicked her shoes off. Agnes moved her hands once more and the sound of conversation drifted up from downstairs.

"Listen!" Agnes said.

The pair fell quiet. They could still hear the muffled conversation downstairs. Agnes raised a finger and the sound became amplified. Now they could hear everything. They sat back and listened. As the conversation continued Mary looked across to Agnes.

"I can't understand a word!" She said.

Agnes moved her finger and the amplification stopped. Now all they could hear was the muffled conversation again.

"Whatever language they were speaking it certainly wasn't English". Mary continued.

Agnes shook her head. "It could be Dutch or Flemish. It certainly wasn't French, that much I do know."

"Whatever it was, the landlady spoke it fluently." Replied Mary.

Agnes nodded her head and thought to herself for a few seconds before speaking. Eventually, she nodded her head as if agreeing with herself.

"We know the gentleman who met his fate out there was foreign."

Mary nodded. Agnes continued.

"The men at the door were foreign."

Mary nodded once more.

"The landlady speaks the language fluently. So, let's make a leap of faith. Suppose they are all linked, not just by language. Perhaps by accident we've stumbled across a place where a small group of foreigners gather."

Mary stood up. She was better thinking on her feet despite them still aching from the shoes she had worn.

"The landlady did say he came two or three times a year."

Agnes looked up at her. "Sit down you're making me nervous!"

Mary ignored her, walked across to the window and looked out over the slipway to sea. She could just make out small boats as they fell and rose on the tide. She turned away and looked towards Agnes.

"Suppose this place is what they call a "safe house"?"

Agnes back looked at her. The girl could be right. She thought for a few minutes.

"A safe house for who, though?"

"The foreigners!" Exclaimed Mary.

Agnes nodded. "But why do they need a safe house. What are they up to?"

The couple fell silent as Agnes thought it over. It made sense. They had turned up at Robin Hood's Bay and simply asked for the best lodgings and, without any hesitation, had been directed here. That meant the lodging must have a good local reputation, one that must have been built up over a long time. The people around here wouldn't recommend just any lodgings to two such "ladies."

Agnes stood up. "I think it's time we asked our landlady for a recommendation as to where we should eat."

Mary looked across the room at her discarded shoes. "You mean we have to keep wearing these outfits?"

Agnes brushed the front of her dress down. "I'm rather enjoying dressing up. I could get used to being a lady!"

Mary struggled to put her shoes back on. "I'm not. This corset is killing me. I feel so restricted." Agnes smiled. She had long passed the age where she cared about the shape she showed the world. She was an elderly lady with all the appropriate lumps and bumps, but she did rather like wearing a bit of finery now and again.

They descended the stairs and Agnes spotted a small brass bell on the dresser in the entrance hall. She gave it a gentle ring and almost instantly the landlady appeared from a side room. She was dressed in black, her face narrow and stern. Mary thought she resembled a crow.

Agnes put on her best smile. "Excuse our disturbing you, but could you please recommend us a suitable place for an evening meal?"
The landlady looked at the two women. "Across the slipway. The Bay Hotel does a very acceptable dinner. The Dolphin may prove a little basic, the locals you know."

As she spoke Agnes listened carefully. She thought she could detect a hint of an accent, but the woman spoke excellent English. She thanked the woman and turned to leave the house. Mary had already opened the front door when Agnes suddenly turned around and addressed the landlady.

"Those foreign men that accosted us as we entered, I do hope your establishment does does not cater to the more common type. I expected to find a more refined guest. Like the gentlemen I met this morning. I haven't seen him lately. Is he still staying here?"

The landlady remained expressionless. Not a flicker of anything crossed her face.

"I'm afraid our gentleman friend had met with a very bad accident." She gave Agnes a hard look as she continued speaking. "No doubt you will hear all about it as you dine. Indeed there will be talk of nothing else. I hope you have an enjoyable meal!" With that she bowed her head slightly, turned, and returned to the room she had emerged from, shutting the door firmly behind her.

Walking across the slipway Mary paused and looked out to sea. The light had dropped and the sunset had happened without them. Now a thin moonlight was shining onto the sea sending out a rippling light that rose and fell across the incoming tide.

"Pretty!" She said aloud.

Agnes smiled. She wasn't sure whether she was in

the company of a colonel's daughter or a very accomplished goverment spy. If it was the latter Mary was good, very good. She was playing her part of a tourist exceptionally well. She followed Mary's gaze and looked out to sea. It was pretty. Spy or Colonel's daughter. "Well," she said to herself, "we'll find out". She turned from the sea and headed towards the ebehind the bar asked. She glanced across the room to the speakers. The question had caused a pause in their conversation. She watched as they just shook their heads slightly and took to their own thoughts.

Then Agnes heard it. It was soft, almost in the background to the burble of conversation that filled the room. She tuned in. It was coming from outside the front door. Someone was whistling, just a few shot notes like the start of a song. They stopped, paused and repeated the phrase once again, a little louder.

She looked around the room. In the corner near the

door two men had obviously heard the tune. They both finished off their drinks in a series of quick gulps and, wiping the residue from their mouths with the backs of their hands they stood up and quickly moved towards the door. Agnes looked across to Mary.

"We need to follow them!" he said quietly and nodded towards the door.

Mary looked down at her dress. "In this?" She asked.

Agnes shook her head. "I have my ways!"

It took the best part of another ten minutes before Agnes paid the bill and walk from the Bay Hotel back across the square, past the slipway and to the door of their lodgings. As they entered the front door the landlady appeared in the hall before them.

"Ladies, I'm so glad I have happened upon you. I

afraid the sudden death of my gentlemen guest has affected the household more than I realised. I need some time to gather my thoughts as well as arrange for his body and effects to be collected."

She paused. Agnes cocked her head. She had an idea where this one-sided conversation was going. She wasn't wrong.

"So it is with the deepest of regret that I must ask you to vacate your rooms the first thing in the morning. I do hope you understand. Obviously, I will refund any monies owing to you."

With that she gave a slight bow of her head, turned and returned back to her private room.

"Well I've been thrown out of better places than this!" Remarked Agnes as she sat heavily on the chair by the window in her room. Mary at on the bed and kicked her shoes off.

"What now?" She asked.

Agnes moved her hands and wriggled her fingers. "Now we can't be overheard, or disturbed!"

"Something's happened!" Mary said as she rubbed her foot.

Agnes looked at her. "Yes it has. A foreign gentleman on some nefarious mission made some sort of delivery and received payment. He was promptly murdered by someone from the same organisation. In short, he was double crossed. So we have two rival factions. I think I can say with some surety that the gentlemen we met at the door are, or were, in cahoots with the dead man, as is the landlady of this establishment. In fact come to think of it I would hazard a guess that this house is the centre of their operations. That's why they want us out of the way. They haven't taken the killing of their man lightly. Some sort of retribution is being planned."

She paused. Mary looked as if she was about to speak. Agnes held up her hand and began to speak again.

"The man wasn't selling rope. Look around, can you see anyone around here bring able to afford new rope in the quantities that would make it worthwhile even visiting here, and don't mention the chandlery. The chandlery here buys directly from Andrew Marks down in Scarborough. Anyway if there was an agent selling rope anywhere between here and Whitby Andrew would know about it and try to put a stop to it. So our man was selling something else, something in small waterproof packages. The ones I saw earlier."

Mary took advantage of a pause. "It sounds feasible. If a group of foreigners is involved that explains why Jack and the Colonel-with-no-name have an interest."

Ages looked up at her. "But can you find a connection?"

Mary shook her head. "No. No yet."

Agnes shrugged. "Maybe. It's a leap of faith, but one I'm willing to take."

She stood up and reached for her bowl. Somehow it was already full of water. Once again she reached into her pocket that wasn't there and pulled out a pinch of herbs and potions that she sprinkled on its surface.

A mist appeared in the water and then cleared. It revealed a small room. It had no windows, the only light coming from a single candle placed on a table in the centre of the room. Sat around the table on rough chairs were six men. Two of them were the men that Agnes had seen leaving the Bay Hotel. In front of them was a flagon and six tankards. In the background, almost hidden deep in the shadows was a black cat. She looked up at Mary and carefully placed her finger upright across her lips. She smiled and the air shimmered. Mary blinked. Where Agnes had been sitting was a very large and puzzled black cat. It didn't look happy at its sudden change in circumstance. It arched its back and dipped its head and then began to lap the water from the scrying bowl. Mary sat back and wondered what would happen if the cat drank all the water. The ramifications were beyond puzzling. Before she could do anything the cat saw what was in the water. Its eyes suddenly widened to the size of saucers and it let out a small growl. It then turned its back on the bowl, curled up in the chair and began washing itself. Mary breathed a sigh of relief and looked into the water, all she could see was six men seated around a table lit by a single candle.

It must have been fifteen minutes later, Mary had just rested her eyes for a moment and when she opened them again she saw Agnes sat in the chair.

She looked around. There was no sign of a black cat.

"Interesting!" Agnes remarked.

Mary waited a full minute before asking. "Well?"

Agnes brushed the front of her dress. "Sorry. I thought I was keeping you up!"

Mary reddened.

"Sorry. Cheap joke!" Agnes said feeling just a little contrite. It had been a long day and the poor girl had suffered from wearing those shoes.

"It seems our six men are a part of a larger gang, one that specialising in import and export, though from what I could gather mainly import. A couple of them were upset at the death of their main supplier."

"And?" Mary asked after another minute of silence.

"The smaller of the men said something that might prove very useful. He said, "The Whistler has his reasons." That was all. The answer seemed to satisfy them and they settled down to finish off the flagon. How was the cat by the way?"

The question took Mary by surprise. "Fine, very cat like I suppose!"

Agnes nodded. "I just thought I'd ask. Sometimes they can get a bit fractious when things like that happen."

Mary was about to ask about the cat trick. For a start, she wanted to know how there came to be two cats, in two different places.

"It's just a trick!" Said Agnes.

Again Mary wondered if the woman could really read minds.

Chapter Three.

Two days later Agnes narrated the story of the events in Robin Hood's Bay to the three people sat around the desk in the office inside Andrew Marks chandlery. Despite Mary having lived it herself she still listened closely as Agnes had noticed things and made connections that she hadn't, and she was meant to be the spy! It was at that moment that Mary realised she did have a lot to learn from the unassuming elderly lady sat opposite her.

As Agnes continued speaking Mary looked at the other two people sat around the table. Andrew Marks was a tall, almost good looking man with a slight nervous twitch, which Mary noticed, only occurred when Agnes was in the room. She also formed the opinion that his prematurely greying hair just might be due to his association with Agnes.

The other person sat at the table was Marmaduke. As she looked at him she half closed her eyes. There was something cat- like about him, especially when he took to lapping his tea from his saucer. He saw her looking and placed the saucer back on the table.

"Bad habit!" He mouthed in her direction.

As he turned from her she noticed his fingernails. They seemed to change shape. "Oh yes!" She said to herself. "Dancing Jack was right. Marmaduke is a very exceptional man!"

She turned her attention back to the conversation. Agnes had stopped talking and Andrew spoke.

"The Whistler?" he shook his head. "Never heard of anyone by that name."

"They signal each other by a whistle?" Asked Marmaduke.

Agnes nodded and whistled the tune. "Then they do it again." She said before adding, "It might be useful if you all learnt it."

For the next few minutes Agnes tried to teach them the refrain, then the pause and then the tune once again. They all quickly learnt it with the exception of Marmaduke. For some reason he couldn't purse his lips properly due to his to canine teeth that, the more you looked at them, looked more like two fangs.

Agnes realised he needed a little help. She moved her finger slightly. Marmaduke pursed his lips once more and repeated the signal perfectly.

"So this Whistler is importing. Our foreign gents are selling. Why suddenly upset the business by killing the supplier? It doesn't make sense." Andrew said.

"More to the point what are they importing?"

Commented Agnes.

Andrew pulled a large ledger towards him and opened it up. He skim read each page, tracing items down the list with his index finger. When he got to the end of the book he shut it firmly and looked up.

"There's nothing here to suggest any irregular shipping. As far as Scarborough goes there's nothing suspicious, and I'm including illicit cargo."

"What about the other harbours along the coast?" Mary asked.

Andrew looked across his desk at her. "I have enough trouble keeping track of what's going on here. I have no idea of what could be going on up Whitby way."

Marmaduke looked around the group. "Of course

we are all assuming that whatever the goods are they came by sea. Suppose our foreign man brought the goods overland?"

That shut everybody up as they revised their opinions.

After a while Andrew nodded. "Marmaduke has a point. Suppose the packets were brought in a trunk as part of his luggage. From what you describe they were small enough."

Agnes slapped her forehead with the palm of her hand. "That thought never crossed my mind. I've been lax. I should have had a look among his belongs while I had the chance."

Andrew shook his head. "From what you saw I would say he arranged the delivery before he collected the proceeds. You wouldn't have found anything, it would have already gone."

Agnes looked at him. "But I might have found a clue!"

Mary leant forward. "Is there any chance we could find out how the man travelled to Robin Hood's Bay?"

Andrew shrugged. "If he didn't arrive at the Bay by sea he must have travelled either from Whitby or here, and I'm sure that no one like him landed here."

"What I meant was, could he have travelled to the Bay by land, from York say?" Mary suggested.

Andrew considered this for a moment and then placed his two hands together and addressed the company.

"The man was carrying something illicit. Somehow he got it into the country, there's nothing to say that he couldn't have landed and brought it in through the docks in London, Bristol, Newcastle, take your pick, there's no shortage of ports, we're an island nation!"

"How about Hull?" Mary asked.
Andrew nodded. "Why not? It would be an easy journey, from Hull to York, from York to Robin Hood's Bay via the Whitby-Pickering road!"

Marmaduke lifted his head. "If he took that route wouldn't he have to pass Saltersgate?"

Andrew nodded.

Marmaduke continued his line of thought. "Why wasn't he simply robbed as he passed through?"

Andrew shook his head. "No, that lot up at Saltersgate are more careful. These days they don't like to get their hands dirty, they rely on others to do the actual smuggling and stealing, they act more as a clearing house. They're well organised and control the distribution."

He paused and looked across the Marmaduke. "And they control it with an iron fist. They operate a strict code. Anyone who gets in their way simply disappears. There's a lot of empty moor up there."

Agnes looked at him. He felt her eyes searching his face. He braced himself for her next question. It wasn't long in coming.

"Andrew, what exactly do you know about Saltersgate and its dealings?"

Andrew knew his only answer had to be truthful. Agnes could spot a falsehood from yards away.

"Not a lot!"

Agnes raised an eyebrow.

Andrew reddened slightly. "It wasn't always that

way. Once, years ago now, as I was establishing the business I did some trading with them. Mutual benefit. Then two or three years ago things changed. The trading stopped. I made inquiries and it seemed a new regime had taken over. They were harder, more vicious. They became a clearing house for goods coming across the moor from Whitby and the Bay, passing it onto York and beyond. I tried to open up some sort of negotiations. The man I sent never returned. Since then they've ignored me and I've ignored them. I try to make sure our paths never cross." He gave a sigh.

Agnes broke her look and nodded slightly. Andrew had been telling the truth.

"Just how hard and vicious are they?"

Andrew looked at Marmaduke and shook his head. "Put it this way. It would take half of the Castle's garrison to attack that place, and when they arrived they would find a legal and fully established inn, complete with landlord who can show a full set of legitimate books and ledgers. Everyone else would have vanished across the moor. They are as impossible to catch as a mist!"

Marmaduke was about to say something when Andrew lifted his hand and continued speaking. "But don't mistake prudence for weakness. They are vicious. Like I say anyone who crosses them, anyone who attempts to betray them, in fact anyone who they take a dislike to is simply removed. Customs and excisemen, smugglers, carters, it makes no difference to them."

He looked across towards Agnes. "Of course we have no direct links between Saltersgate and the events you saw at The Bay."

Mary turned to Agnes. "That's true, but there must be a connection, otherwise why did Jack mention the place?"

Andrew turned to her. "Like I say, the two may not be connected. Perhaps someone else has entered the import-export business, a third party."

Agnes looked out of the office window at the bus harbour and the tangle of ships masts and sails.

"There's too many whys and wherefores, too many questions and not enough facts."

She turned back and looked at the people around the table. "Perhaps the third party is this man called The Whistler."

The room fell silent once again whilst they all thought this through.

Eventually Andrew broke the silence by slapping the palms of his hands on the edge of his desk. "Look we can sit around here pontificating until the end of time, but we still have nothing firm to act on."

He looked at Agnes. "Anyway, why are we doing this, who are we acting on behalf of?"

A sudden noise made them all jump. They looked up to see a figure leaning against the frame of the open office door.

"Actually, old chap, you're acting on behalf of the Crown!"

Mary moved first. She leapt to her feet, ran to the figure at the door and threw her arms around him. The man lifted her up and kissed her on the cheek. Marmaduke smiled.

Andrew rose to his feet.

Agnes looked the newcomer up and down. "If you've ridden from Hull with that wound you'll be needing to sit down. Such a ride could open the wound up again."

Dancing Jack looked down at his side, pulled his jacket to one side and opened his waistcoat. A red damp patch was staining his shirt.

"As usual Agnes you are right. Any chance of a patch up?"

As he spoke he staggered slightly. Mary caught him, preventing him from falling. As she led him to a chair Marmaduke stood up and guided Jack into his own seat.

Agnes turned to Andrew. "I'll need some hot water, fresh linen and that bottle of rum you have in the bottom draw of that bureau over there."

Andrew strode to the door and shouted instructions to his staff manning the chandlery. They scurried off. He walked back and opened the bottom drawer in his bureau. He took put a bottle of rum and placed in the centre of the desk.

Agnes looked up at him "The rum's for me!" she said and turned to Jack. "It's a long time since I did any stitching!"

Marmaduke leant forward and reached for the rum. Andrew gave a cough. Marmaduke gave him a look.

"Do you want a glass with that?" Andrew asked.

An hour later Jack had been patched up. Agnes had tended to the wound, added some herbs she just happened to have in her pocket, given it a slight sprinkle of healing magic and stitched it up.

The man looked up as he fastened his shirt. "Sure I didn't feel a thing. It' a fine sawbones you make Agnes."

Agnes smiled. "You didn't feel anything because I deadened the feeling. When that deadness wears off you'll feel it alright! A couple of days rest and at least you'll be able to ride without bleeding to death."

As Agnes turned back to the desk Jack winced. Marmaduke and Mary pretended they hadn't seen it.
"Jack needs rest. At least a day, possibly more. But I insist on a day at the very least."

She turned towards Mary" To be sure he's not disturbed he'll be staying with me. I suggest we meet in The Mariners in one day's time."

She looked across the desk. "In the meanwhile nobody does anything. Amuse yourselves, talk it over by all means but do nothing until we can talk everything over with Jack. After all, it is his mission!"

There was no arguing with that!

The time was spent productively. Agnes put Jack

into her own bed, moved her hands and fingers and he promptly fell into a deep untroubled sleep. Then she went downstairs but not before sealing the bedroom. She had a lot of secrets in her house and Jack could be very adventurous.

Something was niggling her at the back of her mind. She needed a cup of tea and without thinking, began to dunk Mr. Tetley's finest tea bag up and down in her cup. She knew she was distracted when she realised she had forgotten to pour any water in the cup. She quickly rectified that. As she sipped the brew she looked down at the tea bag. Just a small packet for such a full flavour. She repeated the thought. A small packet for so much pleasure. An image of the packages and the donkey came into her mind.

Small packets and high value. Tobacco? No, too small. Gold? Too light. Gems, too many packages. She dangled her tea bag once more before carrying the cup to the cellar, through the wall and into the twenty-first century.

She sat at her computer and moved her finger The screen sprang into life. As she sat looking at the images she realised that the twenty-first century heat wave was still happening. It was hot in her house. She waved a hand and a cool breeze gently wafted through the building.

"Air conditioning!" She said to the empty room.

Chapter Four

One day later Marmaduke, Mary, Agnes, Andrew and a refreshed Jack were seated around a table at the quiet end of the Three Mariners. They'd fed well. Whitby John and his wife saw to that. Baccy Lad even used a tray to bring their drinks
Agnes looked across to the bar where Whitby John was pretending to polish the bar and Baccy Lad was trying and failing, to find something to do.

"What's the matter with those two?" She asked.

Andrew let out a sigh. "Agnes, they know who you are. They know what you are. They know that Dancing Jack here has an interesting past. They can see that Marmaduke is sat here armed to the teeth, and there's an attractive young lady dressed as a highwayman. They are waiting to see what happens next!"

"So am I!" remarked Mary.

After Agnes had recounted their experience at Robin Hood's Bay and gone through their ideas and their conclusions Jack leant back. Automatically he placed his hand on his wound. To his surprise he realised it wasn't hurting anymore. He glanced at Agnes. She gave him a slight nod.

He leant forward without any pain. "I was tasked with looking for a foreign person. I was given certain information as to his whereabouts in Hull. Mary was with me. Somehow I was compromised, they were waiting or me. Left me for dead."

Mary leant forward. "Who was that woman?"

The intensity of her words surprised everyone. Jack reddened. "An old friend from my days on the road."

Agnes could tell where this particular conversation was going. She cut Mary off before anything else was said.

"Why is this foreign gentleman the subject of the Colonel-with-no-names interest?" She asked.

Jack smiled. "As you know, even as we speak the English and Dutch fleets are facing each other out there."

He nodded in the direction of the North Sea. "Well the Colonel has a bee in his bonnet about Dutch spies. I have a feeling that our man who met his untimely death in Robin Hood's Bay was a spy."

"He can't be!"Remarked Andrew.

Jack raised an eyebrow.

Andrew continued. "First, he wasn't undercover.

He went to a boarding house where he'd stayed before, a place where the landlady spoke the same language and where there were at least five or six of his compatriots. No spy would act like that. This man was a trader, he was dealing in merchandise, not information."

Before Jack could answer Agnes leant forward. "Of course, the dead man might not have been the man Jack was looking for. We still have no idea of how he got to the Bay, and before anyone asks, yes, I have been busy with my scrying bowl."

She chose not to mention the fact that she had spent the last twenty-four hours on her twenty-first-century computer. She also omitted to mention that, despite her technology and modern research tools like Goggle, Wikipedia and hundreds of other websites, she still hadn't found any concrete facts. She had many suspicions and ideas, but no facts, and, as she had learned in the past, suppositions can lead to mistakes, and mistakes can lead to injury, or even worse, death.

She looked up from the table. "I wasn't able to find any trace. I don't even have a name."

"I do!" Replied Mary. "I looked in the landlady's register book. The man's name was Mr. Cuthbert Brodrick. According to his details, he was a rope salesman for a company based in Grantham."

Andrew looked up. "That can't be right. I know that company. I sell some of their rope. It's good. They have some sort of machine that twists the strands together. They supply all manner of customers and shipping lines. I think they might even be supplying the Navy. They're a big company, they wouldn't have a salesman going to Robin Hood's Bay. Not enough profit."

Mary looked deflated.

"It looks like we're back where we started."

Marmaduke said picking a piece of food from between his teeth with a very long finger nail.

"Not quite!" Remarked Jack. "At last we know he wasn't who he claimed to be."

"I wonder if there really is a Cuthbert Broderick?" Mused Mary.

"Probably not!" Replied Agnes. "It was an alias. A cover that allowed him to travel around and do his real business undiscovered."

"And his real business?" Asked Marmaduke.

"He was smuggling. High value, small-item merchandise. I have my suspicions, but the real questions are why was he double-crossed, who by, and who is the Whistler?" Asked Agnes as she looked across to Jack. "And why mention Saltersgate in your message?"

Jack looked around the inn to make sure he wasn't overheard. Over by the door Whitby John and Baccy Lad having polished everything it was possible to polish, were now leaning on the bar, looking in their direction .

Jack lowered his voice. "From what I can gather the gang at Saltersgate provide a distribution network for smuggled goods. For reasons known only to his good self the Colonel-with-no-name suspects they might also be providing a conduit for information."

He leaned back and looked around to see if anyone outside the small circle could have heard. They couldn't.

"What sort of information?" Asked Andrew.

"Governmental!" Replied Jack.

"Spying?" Exclaimed Andrew

Agnes smiled to herself. She noticed that whilst Andrew had no problem with his own distribution of smuggled good and the avoidance of paying Government imposed taxes, he baulked at the idea of spies and treason.

"Whose spies?" Andrew added.

Jack took a deep drink from his tankard and then wiped his mouth with the sleeve of his jacket. "Take your pick. The country is full of them. Benjamin Franklin's sitting in Paris plotting with his French allies, so we have spies from the American colonies and spies from France. Add to that Dutch spies, and probably a few from Spain and Germany, just to keep an eye on things."

Marmaduke looked at him. "And the Colonel thinks that Saltersgate helps these spies?"

Jack lowered his voice once again. "He's sure of it. He's had a man inside their set up for the last two or three years. The only problem is that he hasn't heard from him for the best part of eighteen months or more."

Andrew snorted. "He's dead then!"

"That's what I need to find out!" replied Jack.

Agnes raised an eyebrow. "So how do you propose finding out?"

Jack smiled. "I have the makings of an idea!"

He looked across to Marmaduke. "What say Dancing Jack and Ginger Tom take to the road once again?"

Marmaduke looked across to Agnes.

She just shrugged. "It's as good an idea as any. It's Jack's mission after all."

Andrew gave a short throaty cough. "The two of you are no match for Saltersgate. They'll string you up as soon as look at you!"

Mary looked up from her drink. "There'll be three of us!"

Andrew shook his head. "Two or three. It will make no difference."

Jack looked at him. "Let's not be too hasty Andrew. I'm sure the prospect of handling the ill-gotten gains from three highwaymen might appeal to them."

Andrew shook his head. "Let's just suppose they are happy with the proceeds from their own dealings. Why should they take risks with bothering about some freelance operations?"

Jack smiled. "Because thieves are greedy!"

Agnes leant forward. "Jack is right. However careful they are the prospect of increasing their profits would be of interest to them, but they would have to be sure that such a venture would be worthwhile!"

Jack looked across to Agnes. "I'm sure that a note to the Colonel-with-no-name would enable a suitable robbery to occur nearby. It would have to be a big one mind! Big enough and close enough to attract the attention of them at Saltersgate. When word got around I'm sure they would be only too willing to meet with such people."

Andrew took a drink and examined his tankard as he placed it back on the table. He looked up. "The Colonel would go that far?"

Jack nodded. "Where spies are involved nothing is impossible. The man can move mountains, if they need moving!"

"What about the Whistler and the events we saw up at Robin Hood's Bay?" Asked Mary.

Jack cocked his head to one side. "Well if we search from the opposite end we just might find something that leads us to the Bay. We won't know for sure."

"We'll know if it does, and we'll know if it doesn't. At least we'll know something."

Agnes smiled. The girl was learning.

"How will you get word to the Colonel?" Asked Andrew.

Jack shrugged. "The usual way. I'll go to the nearest garrison, show them a slip of paper and a rider and escort will be dispatched to York within the hour."

Mary raised her face. "He's at York?"

Jack shrugged once again. "I've no idea, but if he's not there someone will make sure the message gets through to him. If necessary they can dispatch a dozen riders to a dozen different places. Trust me. By this time the day after tomorrow at the latest the Colonel will know our plans."

Agnes smiled to herself. She knew how to get a message to him within the hour, but that the army never approved of her magic. Anyway, she could do with a couple of days to put her own ideas into action.

Chapter Five

It was three days later that a young trooper from the Scarborough Garrison entered the bar room of the Three Mariners. He looked around at the inside of the bright, cheerful tavern. Light flooded in through polished windows. Small bunches of freshly picked flowers had been carefully placed inside small glasses on every table. A young man stood behind the bar polishing a tankard. Seated around the fireside were a couple of locals deep in conversation. They stopped talking and looked at the door. When they all saw a trooper standing in the doorway they pointed towards the far end of the bar. The trooper looked to where the men were pointing. Three people were sat there. He gulped. They looked just like the people his mother had warned him about. He took a deep breath, pulled himself erect and marched across to the far table, trying to ignore the actions of the two locals and Baccy Lad who were all throwing mock salutes in his direction.

Despite their familiarity with the army and its formal ways Marmaduke, Jack and Mary were a bit taken aback when a smart young trooper marched across the bar room, stopped at their table, made a snappy salute and asked for a certain Mr. Dancing Jack.

Jack nodded and the trooper took a step towards him, reached into his tunic jacket and pulled out a sealed communication. Mary reached for it but the trooper pulled it away from her.

"Sorry lady, but my orders are to hand it over personal like."

Jack stood up, took the communication and threw the young man a salute. The trooper wasn't used to being saluted, especially by a man who to all appearances was a highwayman. He looked the man up and down. He was wearing a pair of old but sturdy riding boots, a yellow brocade frock coat with a white scarf and a tricorn hat. The trooper also noted that the man in front of him not only wore a sword but had two pistols and very long dagger attached to his belt. In his short army career the one thing he had learnt was not to ask questions. He returned the salute, turned and marched as smartly as he could through the bar and out of the front door trying to ignore that each step he took was accompanied by hand clapping from the other drinkers and the young man behind the bar. As the door shut behind him he hoped no one had noticed his red face.

Jack opened the papers and read their contents. Then he looked up.

"A stagecoach with an escort of troopers will pass along the Whitby to Pickering road the day after tomorrow. We will rob it."

Marmaduke looked back at him. "Won't it look

suspicious if we take the money and there's no fight?"

Jack smiled. "There's a plan!"

"That's good!" remarked Mary.

Two days later three riders were positioned on the brow of a small hill on the top of the moors. They were looking down into a valley where a road wound between trees and stone walls. Jack shifted in his saddle. In front of him was a black, wooden chest he had acquired from Anrew. He leant on it and turned to his companions.

"The inn is two miles down the road. The coach will pass then hit a rut in the road. A wheel will be damaged. They will pull into the inn whilst it undergoes repairs. The army payroll chest will be taken from the coach by six troopers. It will be placed under their guard in a strong room at the rear if the inn."

There was a pause.

"And?" Marmaduke asked.

Jack laughed. "Watch!" He said and pulled his horse around and set off in the direction of the inn.

They approached the building from the rear, dismounted and left their horses tied outside a small stable building. Jack lifted the wooden chest and carefully placed it outside of a back door before they entered. Once inside they found themselves in a dark and dingy corridor from which a number of doors led off. They ignored the doors and went through the door at the end of the corridor ad found themselves in an equally dark and dingy bar room. Once he could make out where it was in the gloom Jack walked across to the bar and ordered three drinks.

They had sat there almost an hour when they heard a commotion outside on the road. They looked out of a small square window just in time to see a coach and horsemen pass by.

"Won't be long now!" Jack said quietly.

It wasn't. Less than fifteen minutes later the door of the inn opened and a trooper entered. He looked around and opened the door wider. Five more troopers entered carrying a black wooden chest. They placed it in the centre of the room and stood by it. A seventh man marched in. He was a sergeant and obviously the man in charge. He marched right up to the bar and demanded in a very loud, parade ground voice, that the landlord provide them with food and drink and a safe room to lodge their chest whilst their coach was being repaired.

The tone of his demand and the look on his face told the landlord that there would be no negotiations. He turned from his bar and invited the sergeant and his men to follow him. He led them out of the back door and into the corridor. Jack looked at Marmaduke and winked.

It was a few moments later that the landlord and the troopers re-entered the bar. The landlord went behind the bar and filled six tankards with ale. Jack nodded and unseen, slipped out of the room and into the corridor.

He hadn't gone halfway down when he came face to face with the sergeant. The man was standing outside a closed door and held his musket in his hand. He raised it chest high as he saw Jack approaching.

"You got the replacement chest?" The sergeant asked.

Jack nodded at the rear door. "It's just outside."

The Sergeant-with-no- name nodded. "Better get it in here sharpish." He said.

Jack opened the rear door. He brought the chest inside whilst the sergeant opened the door behind him and dragged out a second, identical chest. Then two men exchanged the chests and the sergeant examined the weight of the replacement.

He nodded. "Near enough!"

"It should be, I filled it myself!" replied Jack

The sergeant shoved the replacement chest into the room and locked the door whilst Jack dragged the army chest outside and across the yard where he covered it with a pile of old straw. He turned and re-entered the back door. The sergeant was back at his post guarding the door. As he was about to pass him the Sergeant held his arm.

"Message from his nibs. He says every penny is accounted for. Any shortfall is to be made up from your wages."

He then leant forward and in a whisper added. "If you need any cash for pity's sake make sure you get receipts!"

With that he returned to his post and raised his musket. Jack hadn't gone three step before the Sergeant suddenly shouted out.

"Jenkins, Thompson. To me!"

Jack barely had time to get out of the way before two burly troopers burst through the doorway.

The Sergeant-with-no-name barked at them. "Why was this man allowed out here? For all you know he could have planned a robbery. Look at him! Would you trust your family jewels with a man like that? Negligence! Consider yourselves on report. Now stand here. No one enters this corridor until that bloody coach is fixed, even if it takes all night."

As the two unlucky troopers took up positions either side of the doorway Jack walked into the bar and straight across to where Marmaduke and Mary were sitting.

"Time to go!" He said and promptly walked out of the front door.

Marmaduke and Mary drank up and followed him. By the time they had caught up with him he was sat on his horse with the wooden chest resting in his saddle. He waited until they mounted and rode of leading them onto the main road and then onto a small track that led to the open moor. They had travelled around five miles when Jack pulled his horse to a halt.

"Well, that went well!" He said.

Marmaduke shook his head. "There's one thing I don't understand. If by carrying out this daring robbery we're meant to be attracting the attention of the Saltersgate lot, how are they going to know we did it?"

"Not only that," Added Mary. "How are they going to know there's been a robbery at all?"

Jack simply smiled. "Because as it's being put back onto the coach it will fall and break open. A pile of rocks will fall out!"

Marmaduke smiled and Mary laughed. Then she added, "But how will people know it was us?"

"Because five minutes after the chest is opened six troopers and a very angry Sergeant will ride hell for leather down the moorland road asking anyone and everyone they meet about three people fitting our description. By the time they are finished everyone between Whitby and Malton will have heard of the three highwaymen who magicked away an army payroll from under their very noses."

Back in Scarborough Agnes leant back from her scrying bowl. It had gone well, very well in fact. Exactly as she and the Colonel-with-no-name had planned. She smiled to herself. The Colonel, whilst adhering to official army policy of not believing in magic, was open-minded enough to accept that there were things in heaven and earth that he couldn't understand, but if it gave him an edge against his country's enemies, well who was he to turn down an advantage. However, he wasn't sure he could get used to communicating via a bowl of water, and only speaking by way of a combination of lip reading, signs, and written notes held to the water's surface. Still, despite the drawbacks, his life would be a lot easier of he could communicate with every one of his spies like that.

Chapter Six

They had been on the moor all of the night and had bedded down among the heather in a slight depression, building a small fire in a group of stones. As it was high summer the dawn broke early spreading a pale grey light across the moorland.

Marmaduke opened his good eye. He had heard a noise. He had bedded down a few feet away from the embers where the fire had been. Quickly he rolled to one side and tried to flatten his body deep into the heather. His body flexed and flattened into a cat-like shape, His ear twitched. There was the noise again. It was a slight rustling in the heather about twenty yards away. It was hardly audible. He knew that it was only his acute senses that made it possible for him to hear it. His companions couldn't hear it. They slept on. He held his breath and listened. In the distance he heard one of their horses softly whinny. It came from a small clump of trees where they had hobbled them for the night. Then he heard more rustling, then a whispered conversation.

By the sound Marmaduke estimated there were three or four of them out there. He waited. The rustling got nearer. Then, just as dawn sent a shaft of sunshine across the moor, four figures rose out of the heather and charged towards the sleepers with pistols and swords drawn.

They hadn't taken more than a couple of steps before what seemed to the attackers like a creature from hell burst out of the heather at them. As the thing passed through them one man dropped to his knees and felt the hole that had been ripped in his throat. A second man fired his pistol but the shot flew harmlessly across the moor, he looked down with surprise at the dagger sticking out of his chest.

The move had been so quick that the two other men hardly had time to realise what had happened when a second and third shot rang out. The two men fell backwards.

"Anymore?" Jack asked, blowing the smoke from the end of this pistol.

Marmaduke shook his head. "Just the four of them."

Jack walked across to look at the body of the man who had fallen first. He looked down and winced at the severity of the wound and the blood.

"Freelancers or Saltersgate? What do you reckon?" he asked.

Marmaduke shrugged. "Who can tell?"

"Search them?" Mary suggested.

They did.

Apart from some lose coins and an assortment of various knives and daggers, pistols, powder, and shot, there was nothing that identified the men.

"What shall we do with them?" Mary asked.

"Leave them where they are. Someone will find them, eventually." Jack said.

They gathered up their belongings and broke camp. As the new day fully dawned three figures could be seen crossing the open moor to the grove of trees where their horses were waiting for them. They mounted and sat looking across the moor.

"Where to now?" Asked Marmaduke.

"Robin Hood's Bay!" Mary said.

Jack turned to her. "Why on earth would we head

towards the Bay?"

Mary placed her hands on her hips. "Well if we are the highwaymen we're meant to be, clever enough to rob an army payroll right under the noses of the army, surely we wouldn't be so stupid as to march straight into the arms of the well known local gang!"

Marmaduke nodded. "She has a point. Also if we really were aiming to spirit the gold away without being caught, travelling by sea would be preferable to hiding from every army patrol between here and, well anywhere really!"

Jack stroked the back of his horses head. "You do remember we were meant to steal it."

Mary pulled her horse around to face the coast. "Yes but not many people know that. The army will still be looking and, it will save a lot of red faces if they do actually catch us!"

Jack shook his head. "That's the point. The Sergeant-with-no-name is under strict instructions not to find us!"

Mary stood in her stirrups and looked at the far horizon. "Has anyone told them!" She said as she pointed across the moor.

Jack and Marmaduke followed in the direction she was pointing. Now daylight had flooded the moorland hills and valleys they could see a small road winding its way in their direction. In the far distance they could make out movement. Marmaduke shaded his eyes.

"Riders!" he said.

"Riders in army uniforms!" Mary added.

"Robin Hood's Bay it is then." Said Jack and turned his horse in the direction of the sea.

It took an hour before they began dropping down from the moor towards the fields and greenery that led to the steep drop into the villages of Fylingthorpe and down to Robin Hood's Bay.

They spent most of the journey discussing what they should do when they reached their destination. The only thing they agreed on was that they didn't agree. The more they talked the more Mary decided that the two men rarely liked making plans. They preferred reacting to situations, and if there wasn't a situation they would conjure one up. She sighed as she realised she was in the company of men who simply made it up as they went along. A slight shimmer in the air caught her eye. Suddenly a figure appeared sitting on a stone wall some yards in front of them.

As they neared the figure the three riders reined in their horses and stopped. The figure climbed off the wall and stood by the side of the road.

"Why Robin Hood's Bay?" Asked Agnes.

Marmaduke looked at Jack who immediately turned his head towards Mary. She opened her mouth to say something but Agnes raised her hand.

"I take it you haven't eaten yet. Climb down and I'll fix something up."

Jack smiled as he jumped down from his horse. He remembered Agnes's roadside breakfasts from a previous adventure, they were good, very good. The smell of frying bacon taunted his nostrils as he reached up and pulled the wooden chest down from the saddle. He dragged it along the road to the small cooking fire that had appeared and sat down on it.

Agnes split open four freshly baked bread buns and inserted rashers of bacon and a fried egg inside them. Mary watched as she closed them up and passed them around on plates that appeared from nowhere. She looked down at the food, it smelt wonderful. Jack saw her looking.

"Try it. Just make sure the egg doesn't run down your chin."

Mary bit into it, and the egg ran down her chin, but it did taste wonderful.

After they had eaten they sat at the side of the road and let Mary explain her reasoning behind their visit to Robin Hood's Bay. Agnes listened and when Mary had finished she turned to Jack.

"With everything we know about the Bay, and given what happened the last time you visited the place, and add to that the fact that the rumours about a payroll robbery will have reached them, I do hope you are not planning to take the chest of army gold with you."

Jack nodded. "You have the right of it. I was

thinking we should hide it. Bury it and come back for it later."

"Good thinking," remarked Agnes. "Now the three of you just sit here and finish your tea."

She moved her fingers and the air around them shimmered. Everything seemed to stop. Above them a bird froze in mid-air, around them the trees stopped swaying in the wind. The clouds stopped moving across the sky and the shadows on the ground stopped where they were. Agnes looked at the wooden chest, moved another finger and the air around it shimmered. A few feet away, behind the stone wall, a tree seemed to give a little shiver. Agnes moved her hand once again and the air shimmered. The world around them came back to life.

Marmaduke blew on his tea. It was still hot. He looked up. He was sure that a second ago Jack had been sat on the wooden chest. Now he was sat on the ground.

Mary gave a little giggle. First there was a box, now there wasn't. She liked Agnes. Jack looked down with surprise to find he was sitting on the ground. He checked, he hadn't felt a bump, his cup was still full, there wasn't even a ripple on its surface, just steam. He looked across at Agnes. She gave a slight smile.

"It's buried. No one will find it until I am ready for them to find it." She said and looked at Jack.

"Before you say anything you'll find a small pouch in your saddlebag. It's a small portion of the army gold. You'll probably need to flash some around, just enough to be convincing. Oh, and if you spend anything make sure you get a receipt, you'll have to account for it."

Jack cocked an eyebrow at her. "You haven't been talking to his nibs by any chance?" he asked.

Agnes smiled. "That would be telling!"

She stood up and moved her hands. All traces of the fire and breakfast disappeared. She brushed some crumbs from the front of her dress.

"Now you'd better be on your way. Let's see what Robin Hood's Bay has to offer. Oh and try to avoid actually looking for trouble. I'll find you soon enough. I won't be far away."

The air shimmered and a seagull appeared briefly on the wall before taking flight and lazily flapped its way across the moor and down towards the small fishing community.

Jack and Marmaduke had mounted their horses when they realised that Mary hadn't moved. She was still sitting there open mouthed pointing to the empty wall where Agnes had disappeared and the seagull appeared.

"You get used to things like that when you're around Agnes." Jack said.

"Sometimes she changes into an owl, sometimes a falcon, sometimes a crow. We had a lot of trouble with crows once." Commented Marmaduke.

Mary let out a short gasp. "She really is a...."

Jack cut her off. "Don't use the "W" word. She's just Agnes, it's what she does."

As Mary stood up and climbed into her saddle she muttered to herself. "I could just about cope with her changing into a cat. You expect witches to have cats. " Then she remembered Marmaduke. She looked up to see him looking at her. She reddened and kicked her horse into movement.

As they dropped down the steep hill that formed the main street of Robin Hood's Bay they dismounted and led their horses until they came to a small inn that provided stabling. Jack paid the ostler with a coin from the army payroll. A gold sovereign. The ostler looked at it sat in the palm of his hand for a second before lifting it to his mouth and biting down hard on its edge so hard that he hurt his teeth.

"That's on account. I'll expect a bill when I leave." Jack said.

As they walked down the street Marmaduke nudged Jack and nodded further down to where a man stood at the end of an alleyway that led off the main street. The man was watching them. They ignored him and continued down the road heading towards the slipway and the sea. A movement caused Marmaduke to look up. There was a face in an upstairs window looking down on them. They walked past the entrance to a small tavern. They hadn't gone more than a few paces when Jack turned around. The occupants of the tavern were standing at the door looking at them, others peered out from the windows.

"Looks like we are the centre of attention." Jack said quietly.

"Probably something to do with that gold sovereign!" Marmaduke said.

Mary sighed to herself. How the two of them believed that a six foot high, ginger-haired man with one eye and missing a bit of one ear dressed as if he was a one-man war band accompanied by a dandy highwayman would not be the centre of attention was beyond her.

"Money talks!" Replied Jack.

A sudden noise attracted their attention. They turned to see a one-armed man maneuvering a hurdy-gurdy onto the street. It's legs dragged and rattled on the cobbles. The man finally got it into place outside a small shop and turned its handle. A ragged mechanical tune escaped from its sound box. The man looked across to them and kicked a tin cup in their direction. They ignored him and walked on.

Further down the street they were forced into the middle of the road by a woman wearing a wooden yolk carrying two buckets. She looked up at them before turning off into another small alleyway.

At the bottom of the hill, the road opened up into a square where a slipway led to the sea shore. A stream emerged from under the slipway and flowed into the sea. They looked out at a receding tide that revealed a rocky beach covered in clumps of seaweed. They looked around them. To one side was the lodging house where Mary had stayed, opposite it, across the slipway, was The Bay Hotel. One side of it appeared to grow out of the sea, on the other side was a small alleyway between it and the building next door, a small shop selling provisions. A man leant on the doorway looking back at them. The three of them exchanged a look, nodded and headed for the doorway of the Bay Hotel.

As soon as they entered the bar the room fell silent. They looked around at a dozen or so drinkers scattered around a number of small tables. All eyes were on them as they walked to the man behind the bar. Before they had a chance to say anything the man put his hands on the bar top and looked them up and down.

"Don't want no trouble!" he grunted.

Mary looked at him. He had a weather-beaten face, heavily creased. White stubble covered him like a winter's frost. His hair hung long and greasy, as he spoke he wiped his hands on a dirty cloth.

"Don't intend to make any!"She replied.

The man started and looked closer at her, realising

for the first time he was addressing a female.

"Didn't mention no woman!" he said.

Jack smiled. "So we are expected!" he said.

The man looked flustered. He wiped his mouth with the back of his sleeve and walked slowly along the bar. They all noticed he had a slight limp.

"Don't know what you mean!" he said.

Jack reached into his waistcoat pocket and pulled out a gold coin. He flicked it and it spun up in the air before landing on the top of the bar where it began to spin. The man behind the bar slammed his hand on it before it could roll away.

"A bottle of port for a start, and make it a decent one." Jack said

As the man turned to get the bottle Jack walked across the wood panelled room and took a vacant table by a small window that looked out over the sea. As they sat down they were aware that every eye in the place was on them. The three sat and returned the looks. No one held their gaze and the other drinkers began to turn away and speak to each other in hushed whispers. The man behind the bar shuffled across the room and placed an open bottle and three glasses on their table. Marmaduke nodded and the man limped back to the bar.

They had consumed half the bottle when Mary began to notice a change in the room, very quietly a few men had entered the bar and seated themselves around the room. When she counted up to eight of them she tapped Jack on the arm. He gave a slight nod.

"When the landlord leaves the room, be ready!" he whispered.

The words had hardly left his lips when the barman slipped out of a side door. There was a grating noise and they turned to see a wooden panel in the far wall slide open. Three men slipped out heavily armed with pistols and swords, as they stepped inside the room other men stood up. Two went to the door and stood either side of it. Jack leant back in his seat and looked up at the newcomers.

"Can I help you gentlemen?" he asked politely.

One of the three men stepped forward. He was tall and thin-faced with long lank hair that fell onto a stained leather jerkin fastened with a broad leather belt. Across his face was a scar running from the temple down the side of his face giving the appearance that half of his face was fixed in a permanent smile. He held his pistol out in front of him, directly at Jacks' chest.

"Now how about you slide your pistols over that table there careful like and tell me who you are?"

Very slowly and deliberately the three of them pulled their pistols from their belts and slid them over the table. Jack looked at the pistol pointed at him.

"My name is Dancing Jack, to my right and left are my travelling companions, Mean Mary and Ginger Tom. You may have heard the names."

The man holding the gun remained expressionless. "Might have, there again, might not have. What's your business here?"

Jack shrugged. "Just passing through!"

The man moved his pistol from one to the other. "From where to where?"

Jack leant further back in his seat. "From here to there!"

The man levelled his pistol at Jack's head. "I ain't

playing games!"

Jack smiled. "My dear sir, I never for a moment thought you were. However your boss is curious, you've been sent to find out if we are the gentlemen of the road that's currently being looked for all over the moors by half the English Army. He will be very annoyed if you kill us before he has his answer. I do advise you to think most carefully. Is it a really good idea to kill the only people who know where the army gold is?"

The man holding the gun gave a tight-lipped, forced smile. "Think you're smart do you?"

He moved his pistol so it pointed at Mary's head. "I can shoot either of your companions. Now talk, what are you doing here?"

Jack sighed. "If you must know I thought it would be a good place to lie low. The army's searching the moors. I figured we'd give them a couple of days to get bored and then slip away unseen."

The man holding the pistol gave a small harsh laugh." It ain't as easy as that. There's dues to be paid. Compensation like. We've had to delay our own business whilst the army's out there. We have our own deliveries to make."

Jack laughed out loud. "Oh don't tell me we've upset the local smuggling gang. Now that would be too ironic!"

The man was about to say something when he was interrupted by a sound from the hidden passageway. I was someone whistling the first line of a tune. The man with the gun turned towards the open panel. He pursed his lips and whistled. The signal was answered and the hidden figure whistled a second art of the tune. The man with the gun turned into the room and barked an order.

"Leave us!" he said and waved his pistol in the

direction of the door.

The men in the bar stood up and, without a word, filed out of the room leaving just the three armed men. As the door closed behind them another figure appeared at the open panel. It was a man dressed in a long riding coat. He wore a low brimmed hat pulled down over his head. Across his face he wore a black scarf. He raised a gloved hand to speak.

"My friends, congratulations. You have succeeded in an audacious robbery. Luck must have been with you. Unfortunately, when you entered here it deserted you."

Without warning Jack suddenly leant back and kicked the table over. As it crashed to the floor the three of them leapt either side of it. The unexpected movement caught the three armed men by surprise. Two of them discharged their weapons, missing their targets.

As Mary made her move she spun around, drew her dagger and slashed the nearest man across the midriff. As she continued her spin a second dagger appeared in her hand and plunged into the side of the second man.

Marmaduke sprang at the masked man. With one sweep of his hand he removed the man's mask and scraped large gouges out of the side of his face. The man screamed and fell to his knees.

"Bolt the door!" Jack shouted.

Mary bounded across the room and slid a bolt across the door. For good measure she dragged a table behind it. It was secure enough.

Jack pulled out his own dagger and gently poked into the neck of the scar-faced man. A trickle of blood appeared. The man began to sweat.

Marmaduke bent down and dragged the unmasked

man to his feet. He looked at the wounds he had inflicted. The cuts were superficial, the man would live.

"You're not the Whistler!" he said to the man.

The man whimpered. "I never said I was!"

"You whistled. You pretended. You thought we'd be frightened of the Whistler!" Marmaduke snarled in the man's face.

Mary stepped forward. "You thought you could frighten us into sharing the money by pretending you were the Whistler?" She shook her head in amazement. "Stupid man!"

"It was the wrong tune!" The three of them said together and then laughed.

Jack turned to the man. "Now tell me who you are otherwise this dagger might just slip and that wouldn't prove to be too healthy, at least for you!"

The man tried to pull his head away but found that he already has his back against the wall. He had no choice, he started to speak.

"We're just locals. Smugglers, a bit of robbery. Don't mean no harm. If the stories are true it was worth a chance."

Jack shook his head in disbelief. "It amazes me that anyone would be so stupid enough to think I'd walk around with a chest full of army gold just waiting to be robbed." He moved the dagger and another trickle of blood appeared running down the man's neck.

Marmaduke was still holding his man by the neck. He moved his face closer to his captive's face and let out a low growl. The man's eyes widened as he saw Marmaduke's teeth. They were fangs. He shook and promptly wet himself.

"Talk!" Marmaduke said and let go of the man. The man fell back and stumbled.

Jack turned to Mary. "You'll notice that Marmaduke likes the direct approach. He never beats around the bush."

The man with the dagger at his neck looked around him wondering just who or what these people were. He began to speak "We thought we'd try to rob you. Everyone's on the lookout for you. Three highwaymen who stole the army payroll."

Marmaduke stood over him. "We know that. Tell me something I don't know. Tell me about the Whistler!"

Both of the men glanced at each other. Jack twitched his dagger a fraction of an inch. The man in front of him wriggled.

"Don't know who he is. No one knows, even his

own men don't know his identity. Him and his gang showed up a couple or so years ago now. At first we all thought he was linked to Saltersgate."

Marmaduke interrupted him. "What's Saltersgate?"

The two men glanced at each other once again. The man with the dagger at his throat gave a small laugh. "If you don't know about Saltersgate you must be leading a charmed life. They handle all the stolen goods around here. They have connections. Whatever you've got they'll either buy it or arranged transportation. "

The man on the floor tried to stand. Marmaduke trod on his hand. "Do you buy and sell with them?"

The man grunted and remained on the ground. He looked up at Marmaduke. "Everybody does. If you want to shift anything you have to go through them."

The man in front of Jack spoke. "They'll be looking for you. They won't let a robbery like yours happen on their patch without getting involved. Stands to reason, they'd lose face."

"It must have been them last night!" Mary said. The two prisoners cast another glance at each other. Jack spotted it.

"Do you know anything about an attack on us last night!"

"This morning actually!" remarked Mary.

Both men shook their heads.

Marmaduke lifted his foot and released the man's hand and squatted down on his haunches to face him. He pulled back slightly as his nose was assaulted by the smell of urine.

"Finish telling me about the Whistler. What does he trade in and what's his relationship with Saltersgate?"

The man now had a very close up look at Marmaduke's fangs and he began talking. "His gang do some robbery's here and there, that's all I know. As far as Saltersgate's concerned they have an arrangement. They keep out of each others business."

"Where can we find this Whistler?" Mary asked.

The man twisted his head around to face her. "You don't. He finds you!"

Jack withdrew the dagger his dagger and the man let out a sigh of relief.

"Get out, both of you, and take your dead with you. When people ask, tell them you were foolish enough to try to rob Dancing Jack. Remember the name and the face. If I see your face again I will be the last thing you see. I will kill you!"

The man helped his comrade to his feet and looked around them.

"You'd better use the main door". Jack said.
As the two men began to drag the bodies of their men towards the door, Jack fumbled inside his coat. He seemed to be searching for something. Suddenly he gave a little smile and pulled out a small tube. The tube has a fuse on it. Marmaduke raised an eyebrow. Mary's mouth fell slightly open.

"Is that..?" She asked.

Jack nodded and looked down at the tube in his hand. "Not much but big enough to make a bit of a bang. Enough to make a door open."

He looked across at Marmaduke. "You never know when you might need to get out of a tight situation!"

The two would be robbers had dragged the bodies to the front door and were now standing there speaking in hushed whispers to the men standing outside. The general opinion of who was to re-enter the bar and kill the three outsiders. The man with the scarred face looked back into the room. Mary and Marmaduke were standing there holding two pistols each.

Marmaduke smiled, making sure his fangs were visible, "The first four through the door will die. Then Jack will kill the next two. That's six down and no one's entered the room yet. How many are you, ten? That's only four left."

He moved his hand. No one saw what happened next. All the men knew was that two throwing knives had embedded themselves in the framework of the door. They were less than an inch away from the man with the bleeding throat.

Marmaduke shook his head. "You'll all be dead in less than a minute. Now go away, bury your dead, and get drunk. Just don't ever get in my way again."

As he spoke he gave another cat like growl. No one standing by the door failed to see the fangs that appeared at the side of his mouth. They left. As the door closed behind them Marmaduke turned just in time to see Jack place one end of the tube to a candle flame. The fuse began to fizz and spark. He blew on it as if to encourage it and walked across to the open panel. Without looking he tossed the dynamite into the secret passage and shut the panel.

They had just got through the door when a muffled explosion blew the wooden panelling back into the room followed by a cloud of dust, dirt, and smoke.

Then there was a rumbling sound. Then a crash closely followed by another crash. Mary looked away from the entrance to the inn across the bridge to the slipway. Something wasn't right. She looked again and then tugged Marmaduke's arm. As he turned she pointed. Between the bridge and the slipway a large hole had appeared in the ground. Bricks and stone and mud were falling into it. All around them the fishermen and others turned to look. Fishermen dropped their nets. Tradesmen stopped trading. Two lady shoppers stopped shopping. One fainted.

Across the road an elderly lady wrapped in an old shawl stopped watching a group of men standing outside the boarding house and looked across to the slipway. She watched as three highwaymen ran from the tavern doorway and looked down into the hole.

"Clowns!" She muttered to herself. Then she

noticed a group of men dragging and carrying two dead men away from the scene.

"Deadly clowns!" She added.

Chapter Seven

That night four people gathered around a camp fire built on the edge of a cliff. Below then they could see the twinkling lights of Robin Hood's Bay. The camp was comfortable, Agnes had made sure of that. There were four comfortable easy chairs, cushions and a large pot of something that smelt so good their mouths watered. As they ate Agnes noticed that Mary didn't seem relaxed, that she kept looking this way and that way. Agnes smiled.

"Relax, no one can see us. I've shielded the camp To anyone standing outside we're simply not there."

She turned to Jack. "Now explain to me just why you thought that blowing up one of their secret tunnels and half their slipway was a good idea?"

Jack shrugged. "Just a spur of the moment thing. It'll give then something else to think about apart from us."

Agnes nodded and helped herself to a second helping from the pot. "Oh, it will. You managed to blow up their main tunnel. The one that runs from the sea to the town. The one they use to transport contraband from the beach. You've just made a lot of people's lives very difficult!"

Jack looked across to her. "Is that a bad thing?"

Agnes shrugged. "I've no idea. They do what they do. I'm no judge."

She looked across the three of them. "There have been developments by the way."

They looked across to her from the comfort of their chairs as the stars shone brightly over their heads.

"I popped in to see Andrew earlier. He tells me Salmon Martin was out fishing last night, he was up from Scarborough, around Cloughton way. He reported seeing a large ship standing at anchor about a mile offshore. Boats seemed to be ferrying men ashore."

"Smugglers?" Asked Mary

Agnes shook her head. "No, Andrew says the Salmon Martin swears it was a warship. He thinks it might have been Dutch!"

Jack leant back in his chair and gave a low whistle. Agnes continued. "Not only that but the foreign men I saw here last time were back at the lodging house. I have a feeling someone knows about the death of the rope salesman and have come to ...." She paused to lick her spoon.

"Find out what happened?" Asked Marmaduke as the pause continued.

Agnes looked up from the spoon. "No, by the look of it I would say they are looking for retribution. I took the liberty of flying over them. They are camped two miles down the coast. If you ask me those Dutch men are hardened fighters. They are not in uniform, but you can tell. I think the Dutch army have sent a small force. I think we're been invaded!"

That shut them all up.

Eventually it was Mary that broke the silence. "Why would the Dutch Army be interested in what's happened at Robin Hood's Bay."

Suddenly Jack leant forward and slapped his hands on the arms of his chair. "Mercenaries!" he said.

They all turned to look at him.

"They came off a Dutch ship!" Mary said.

Jack shook his head. "Not necessarily. That fleet out there is made up of all sorts of captains, half of them are pirates. Offer them enough money and they'll accept any commission going."

Agnes gave a little grunt. "It's been five or six days since the incident with the foreign gentleman. How did they find out so quickly and have a force all ready and waiting?"

Jack sat back and absently chewed a finger nail as he thought it through.

Mary looked across at Agnes. "Those men were foreign. Where did they come from? Perhaps this ship isn't part of the Dutch fleet. Perhaps it's been out there all along. Perhaps they are using the fleet as a convenient cover!"

"Perhaps it's how the men got here in the first place." Marmaduke looked towards Jack. "Perhaps they are aware the ports are being watched and they can slip in and out of the country in smaller places known to smugglers."

Jack slapped his forehead with the palm of his hand. "Of course."

Agnes sat back. "Jack, inside a week you've gained a reputation in these parts. Local gangs are dying in an attempt to relieve you of the army gold you've stolen. There's a party of foreign mercenaries arrived to find out who killed their man and you've blown a hole in the centre of their square. Remind me, weren't you meant to be making contact with someone at Saltersgate?"

Jack reddened slightly and gave a sheepish smile. "Circumstances Agnes, circumstances. Anyway, the mercenaries are after the Whistler and his men. They don't know about me!"

Agnes shook her head. "Oh yes they do. Or will. I'm sensing that their men at the boarding house will be most eager to mention three characters who blew a slipway up."

Mary gazed up at the stars. "So what do we do now?" she asked the universe.

"I have an idea!" said Jack

Marmaduke gave a little groan.

Agnes shook her head. "Before we make any further moves in this particular game let's take a few moments to see what moves the other players are planning!"

The three of them were warm, well fed and comfortable. The last thing any of them wanted just now was to stand up, let alone go haring off into the moors once again. They agreed with Agnes and settled down deeper into their chairs and watched as Agnes placed her scrying bowl on a small table placed between the four of them.

Mary looked twice at the table. She could swear it hadn't been there
before. Marmaduke saw the expression on her face.

"You'll get used to it!" He said.

Mary wasn't too sure about that.

Agnes sprinkled her concoction of herbs and spices over the water and after it had fizzed a bit it began to clear. The four of them leant forward to peer into the bowl.

The first thing they saw was the slipway. A series of lanterns illuminated the area, shining bits of light on a number of men working, dragging away broken stone and rubble and clearing away the entrance to a passageway that seemed to lead into the ground and up towards the houses. A horse and cart stood nearby loaded with timber.

"It looks like they are going to shore it up!" Jack remarked.

Agnes said nothing but moved her hand and the vision expanded. She pointed to one side of the slipway where a group of men were standing at the entrance to the alleyway at the side of the boarding house. They seemed to be watching the work.

"It's the foreign men we saw earlier." Exclaimed Mary.

Marmaduke pointed further up, at a different part of the vision. They followed his finger nail. Just up the street, hidden by behind some buildings and sheds were another group of men. They seemed to be hiding and moving in ones and twos from one dark patch to another. To all four of them it was obvious that they were attempting to creep up on the foreigners.

"This should prove interesting!" Agnes commented.

They all watched as the second set of men continued creeping down the series of alleyways and passages until they were at the top of a flight of stairs which led down to the side of the boarding house.

"Should we do something?" Mary asked.

Agnes shook her head. "Until we know a bit more about what's going on I suggest we leave them to it."

As she spoke there was movement at the front of the boarding house. The door opened and the landlady emerged. She shouted something and held the door open. The group of men turned and began running until they reached the safety of the house and entered. The door shut behind them.

It was just in time. As the door closed the second group of men ran down the stairs with daggers and swords drawn. They came to a halt at the front of the boarding house and looked around them. Apart from the men working on the slipway the place was deserted.

"She must have a look out at the rear of the house." Remarked Jack.

Agnes moved her hands and the observers found themselves looking down on the boarding house. The roof seemed to disappear and they were looking inside the building. The first thing they saw were two armed men situated in the attic. One was at the front of the building looking out at the slipway. The second was sat in a chair looking out of a rear window.

"Lookouts!" Remarked Marmaduke.

"There must be another!" Mary remarked.

Marmaduke looked up at her.

She looked back. "Because the two men haven't had time to run downstairs, warn the landlady and get back up again!"

Jack nodded. "Makes sense!" he said.

They looked back into the water to see the men from the alleyway being ushered down a flight of stairs into a cellar. As they entered the lit cellar the watchers saw a door in the far wall. The landlady walked to it, unlocked it and opened it up revealing a passageway. They could see that the passage led up the hill leading towards the centre of the town. A few yards inside the tunnel second passageway opened up. The escaping men took this one and, after a few minutes they reappeared through a small doorway into another alleyway that led to a small track that led out of Robin Hood's Bay and up the cliff, towards the place where they were camped.

"They are coming our way!" Marmaduke observed.

"Don't worry, they won't see us." Agnes said.

She moved her hands and the vision in the scrying bowl returned to the boarding house. It scanned from room to room. They found the landlady seated in a back parlour in a large chair to one side of the fireplace. By the glow of the blaze they could see she wasn't alone. Two men were seated in easy chairs at the other side of the fireplace. Agnes looked closely at them. They both seemed to be well dressed and, by the way they held their delicate cut glass tumblers of port, looked affluent. They were talking and she tried to read their lips. She couldn't. She looked up at the other.

"They are speaking a foreign language!"

Jack leant forward trying to see their lips move. He couldn't and turned to Agnes.

"Is there any way we can tell what they are saying?"

Agnes gave him a look. The air around her shimmered and she simply wasn't there. Instead a seagull gave a flap of its wings and rose up into the night sky before swooping down the hill towards the village and the lodging house.

The gull landed on the wall behind the house. The air shimmered and the gull disappeared. In the dark no one could see the mouse that ran down the wall and squeezed into the house through a slightly open window. Once inside it scampered across a stone flagged floor, through an open door and scuttled into a tiny hole in a skirting board. It emerged at the rear of an elegant back parlour. At the far end of the room, by the fireplace, sat the three people she has seen in her scrying bowl. She settled back on her haunches. The mouse twitched a whisker and suddenly Agnes could hear and understand every word they spoke. The first words that reached her were spoken by the landlady.

"I will not have my people put into danger. You just witnessed what happened, they are becoming hunted men!"

One of the men seated by the opposite side of the fire gave a polite cough.

The second man looked across the room. "I am told by my spies that trouble has broken out between our friends at Saltersgate and a local organisation run by some character called the Whistler."

"It is a local problem!" The first man replied.

The landlady patted her knees with the palms of her hands. "But why kill Jakob, he was only a go-between?"

"He had the money. Perhaps it was only for the

money!"

The woman stood up and shook her head. She looked down at the two seated men. "No, Jakob arranged the shipment. He oversaw the delivery. He collected the money. Then he was killed. How did anyone other than the people he dealt with, know who he was?"

She didn't give them time to answer. She spun around and as she spoke began pacing up and down the room.

"I've had time to think. He was double crossed. Somehow our buyers were in the pay of the Whistler."

One of the men rose to his feet. "Back home they are worried about our security. Men have been dispatched. They will search for this Whistler and his men."

"No doubt it was his men that were outside just then."

The woman turned to face him but the man raised his hand and continued speaking. "I fear we have but two choices. We either neutralise this Whistler or if that proves too problematic, we switch operations. We close down here and open another delivery point, somewhere further north. Scotland maybe!"

The woman sniffed in scorn. "It took a lot of time to establish this route. It will take a year at least to remove and re-establish ourselves."

The first man interrupted her. "Which is why the first option is the more preferable, besides I'm sure our friends at Saltersgate would appreciate the removal of a thorn from their side."

The second man leant forward. "One question puzzles me. That is why has the Whistler suddenly turned his attentions to us? Could it be he knows of our distribution and the part Saltersgate plays? They are being paid well. Perhaps by striking at us he really means to harm them."

The woman stopped her pacing to think about that scenario. She looked back across the room at the two men.

"Gentlemen, it is obvious he has infiltrated our buyers. Somehow he persuaded them to betray Jakob. Why can only be down to speculation, but if we wish to continue our enterprise we must establish contact with the people at Saltersgate."

One of the men brushed at his knees before looking up. "Madam, that is why we are here. As I said, men have been dispatched. They have landed and will arrive soon. With their help we will contact Saltersgate and deal with this Whistler in one operation."

Inside the skirting board Agnes had heard enough. The mouse scurried out of the house the way it had arrived.

The air shimmered and Agnes re-appeared in her chair at the side of the fire in the luxury encampment.

Chapter Eight

Agnes's sudden appearance caused Mary to spill the drink she was nursing on her lap.

"You'll get used to it!" Marmaduke said.

Mary shook her head as she brushed the spilt drink from her leggings. Agnes ignored her and repeated the gist of what she had overheard.

Jack looked thoughtful. "So they bring in contraband and it goes to Saltersgate. No doubt the transactions are not one way. These are not ordinary smugglers."

Mary interrupted him. "Could this be the spy ring that the Colonel-with-no-name sent you to discover?"

Jack looked over to her. "I was just coming to that conclusion."

"They are Dutch by the way!" Agnes said suddenly.

"How do you know for sure?" Asked Mary.

Agnes fumbled in her skirt and pulled out a small coin. She flicked it across the space between her and Mary.

"I got this in some change in that tea shop. To be honest I'd forgotten all about it. It's Dutch. Someone either cheated the cafe owner or made a genuine mistake. The cafe owner simply did what every shop keeper does when they are passed foreign coins, they try to pass them off on the next unsuspecting customer."

Mary tossed the coin to Jack who caught it and examined it closely. He looked up at Agnes. "I've never seen a Dutch coin before, but I'll take your word for it."

Marmaduke stretched. "So who is this Whistler character and why has he suddenly turned up?"

"Let's find out!" Said Jack.

They all looked at him. He shrugged. "By now word will be all over the moor about the three highwaymen who robbed an army payroll and blew up Robin Hood's Bay. I have a feeling he might be interested in meeting us."

He paused and whistled a little tune. "Anyway, we know his password."

"Do you think he has any idea that a small army of mercenaries are after him?" Mary asked.

Jack smiled. "We'll tell him!"

The following morning there was no sign that Agnes's magical camp had ever existed. Not even a blade of grass was broken. As dawn broke over the horizon three riders made their way towards Fylingthorpe and onto the moors beyond. Above them a seagull hovered in the air currents before turning and swooping down towards the small town to lose itself among the roofs and chimneystacks. Agnes preferred the watching game.

The riders had ridden through the village and were on the moor when Marmaduke spotted three figures striding across the road in front of them. They were dressed roughly and wore swords and pistols tucked into thick leather belts. He turned in his saddle and looked behind him. Three more mounted men were following them.

"About time!" Jack muttered.

Marmaduke reached inside his jacket and stroked

the handle of one of his throwing knives. Mary cocked her pistol.

"Easy everyone!" Jack whispered. Then he whistled the tune.

The three men in front of them looked quickly at each other. They did not expect to hear their own password.

"Right tune!" Whispered Mary.

As they pulled their horses to a halt one of the men stepped forward and whistled the next line of the tune. He stared hard at Jack.

"Who are you?" he said.

"Someone with some news for the Whistler." Jack replied.

"Why don't you tell me? I'll decide whether he

should know or not."

There was a blur of movement and the two men either side of the speaker were suddenly on their knees screaming in surprise and pain as they looked down on the two throwing knives that appeared sticking in their thighs. One man began to pull it out whilst the other pulled a pistol.

There was a discharge and the man found himself looking down at his empty hand. It was bleeding. The gun had been blown away along with his trigger finger. As he fell onto the ground Mary blew the end of her smoking pistol.

It all happened so fast that the riders behind them didn't have time to react. Jack had turned his horse around and faced them and before they could reach for their weapons, they found themselves looking down at the ends of two pistols.

Jack waved one of the guns and the riders turned

their horses and retreated back down the road. Jack turned back to the man standing in the middle of the road.

"We'll do the deciding!" he said quietly. "Now take us to the Whistler."

The man shrugged. "Can't!" he said.

"We don't know where he is!" said the man on the floor still trying to slide the knife from his thigh.

"I was afraid you were going to say that!" Jack said as he waved his pistol towards the side of the road. "Over there and sit on the ground. Throw all your weapons as far as you can, Oh and you'd better check on your friends. Ginger Tom here would like his knives back."

As the man did as he was asked Mary turned to Jack. "What now? We can't go on fight after fight. One of them might get lucky!"

Marmaduke gave a slight growl at the man who passed his knives up to him. The man jumped back in surprise as Marmaduke checked the blades and wiped them on his leggings and slid them back inside his jacket.

He looked at Mary. "The Whistler knows what's happened here. There was someone watching from the crest of that hill. They've gone now. We don't have to do anything, we just wait here."

They didn't have to wait long.

Some twenty minutes later a group of men cantered across the moor and joined the road in front of them. They stopped some yards away. Words were exchanged between them before one of the riders pushed his horse forward. As he approached them Marmaduke noticed that the rider wore a mask over his face.

Jack watched as the rider came closer and then

whistled the tune. The rider whistled back.
They watched as the figure rode nearer and nearer slowing his horse to a standstill alongside Jack. The nearer he came the more Marmaduke and Mary gripped their pistols. The man wouldn't have time to draw his before he was shot down. The man glanced at their pistols. He knew that. Slowly he raised his hand palm upwards and then quickly pulled down his face mask to reveal a craggy unshaven face with a scar running down the right side of his face. He raised his head and looked right at Jack.

"By Patrick and all the Saints in Ireland! You took your time getting here Jack!"

No one said a word. Marmaduke looked at the Whistler, then at Mary and finally at Jack. Mary looked at Marmaduke, then at the Whistler and finally at Jack. They saw a slight smile break over his face.

"I thought you were dead!" He said.

As he spoke the Whistler reached up and took his hat off. He turned it upside down and began to fumble inside it. Eventually, he found what he was looking for, pulled it out and handed it to Jack. Jack took it and looked down. In the palm of his hand was a small carved token. Jack held it up to Marmaduke who simply nodded. Jack turned and flicked it through the air at the Whistler. He caught it and replaced it into his hat. Jack turned around.

"Meet O'Flynn, my man inside Saltersgate." He said to the others.

The Whistler shook his head. "Not anymore I'm afraid."

Jack looked him in the eye. "We need to talk. Is there anywhere around here we can go?"

O'Flynn also known as The Whistler smiled.

"There's an inn some miles back in Fylingthorpe, I know the landlord, we'll go there."

The party now plus one turned their horses and returned across the moor back in the direction they had just left. Behind them a group of men that were in the pay of the Whistler followed.

The inn left a lot to be desired. It was dark, dingy and dank with old damp straw covering the earth floor. The landlord showed them to a table at the darker end of the building. As they settled themselves into rickety wooden seats the man brought four tankards of ale to the table.

As he placed them on the table O'Flynn handed him a coin. "That will keep him out of the way for an hour or two. My men will remain outside so we won't be disturbed."

They remained silent and listened as O'Flynn told his story. It was long and detailed. He told how it had taken many months for him to gain the confidence of the men at Saltersgate. He did it bit by bit. Doing some robbery here and there, doing some house breaking and passing the proceeds through them. In exchange he received a portion of the profits. Eventually he expanded and attracted a group of men around him.

He looked up into Jacks' eyes. "I got myself trapped Jack. The more I was accepted the more I robbed, the more I robbed the more men came to me, and the more men that came to me the more of them talked. I went so deep undercover that, in order to protect my identity I became the Whistler."

Jack was about to speak when O'Flynn raised his hand. "Oh come on Jack, what else could I do? You were silent, I would never be fully accepted as a part of Saltersgate. I was stuck between the pair of you so I became an independent operator."

Jack returned the man's look. "There was no way you could get a message to me?"

O'Flynn shrugged. "I thought about it but it was too risky. No one around me that I could trust." He paused and gave a sheepish grin. "Anyway, I was having too good a time!"

"You were meant to be on a commission!" Jack stated.

O'Flynn leant back in his chair "Oh yes, the commission. I can confirm that the Dutch are using contacts at Saltersgate to pass information backwards and forwards. They have an intelligence unit somewhere in Robin Hood's Bay."

Mary was about to speak but as she opened her mouth she received a sharp kick on the shin. She shut her mouth again.

O'Flynn didn't notice but kept on talking. "Like I

said they deal with Saltersgate. The Dutch supply high-quality contraband and they pass on information."

"What information?" Asked Marmaduke.

O'Flynn shrugged. "I never got that close!"

"So what happened in Robin Hood's Bay?"

Jack glanced at Marmaduke and then returned his gaze at O'Flynn. "Marmaduke likes to get straight to the point." He said.

O'Flynn looked at Marmaduke. "It's a fine set of teeth you have there!" he said.

Marmaduke grinned allowing his fangs to show to their fullest. O'Flynn gave a little shudder and looked back at Jack. "Strange company you keep Jack!"

Jack shrugged. "We live in strange times O'Flynn!" he replied.

"Why did you have the foreigner killed?" Asked Marmaduke trying a different approach.

O'Flynn looked to say something but changed his mind and just shrugged. "He was a spy and I needed the money to finance my operations. Men need paying!"

Jack leant forward. "You know the Colonel will want full reports."

O'Flynn smiled. "Ah now Jack, some thing's are better not written down. Anyway from what I hear you've got yourself a nice little haul."

Jack spoke carefully and distinctly. "The robbery was arranged. Every penny is accounted for!"

O'Flynn let out a short laugh. "The Colonel would

go that far to help you get noticed?"

Marmaduke gave a short low growl. "It worked. You're here. Now we know what's going on!"

Mary suddenly spoke "Was it your men on the moor the other morning?"

O'Flynn nodded. "Not my idea, but they were my lads. They got ambitious, thought they'd go freelance. They paid for that mistake."

"What about the men in Robin Hood's Bay?" She continued.

O'Flynn shook his head, took a drink and looked over the edge of his tankard at her. "Locals, amateurs, chancers! They thought they could frighten you into giving up the money, or at least a portion of it. Like I said, amateur chancers!"

"How did you know the man was a spy?" Jack

asked.

O'Flynn stood up and walked to the deserted bar. He found an empty tankard, held it under a spigot and poured himself another drink. He held the tankard up to his nose, sniffed and pulled a face. He walked back to the table.

"The man was not what he pretended to be. He was not a rope seller. I first saw him some six months past. He met with certain representatives from Saltersgate and a transaction was undertaken. Then he went away again. I've no idea where but I managed to follow the transaction. It was moved from Robin Hood's Bay to Saltersgate. Once it was there it was broken down into smaller packages and dispatched inland by various couriers."

"Where inland?" Jack asked.

O'Flynn shrugged "Everywhere. York, Leeds,

Sheffield, Manchester."

A penny dropped and he suddenly looked up at the three of them. "You don't know what the contraband is do you?"

The three of them shook their heads.

O'Flynn took a deep drink from the tankard, winced and looked up. "Opium!" he said.

A silence fell over the table as each one of them absorbed the information. Marmaduke was the first to speak.

"Opium in and information out!"

O'Flynn pushed his tankard away from him. "I figured that by disrupting their operations I could cause them a few problems."

"Oh, you've done that all right!" Jack remarked.

"Even as I speak there's a small platoon of Dutch mercenaries landed just down the coast. They are under orders to eliminate the Whistler and his gang and re-establish the distribution chain."

O'Flynn didn't say anything for a few seconds. Then he gave a short laugh. "Well, Jack my boyo, It looks like you've arrived just in time. What do you suggest?"

Marmaduke was about to make a remark along the lines that what O'Flynn had started he should be ready to face when the door behind him opened and an elderly lady walked into the inn.

O'Flynn leapt to his feet and shouted outside. "I said we were not to be interrupted!"

The elderly lady looked at him with one of those looks. For some reason O'Flynn found himself leading the lady by the arm towards the table where he pulled out a chair and invited her to sit down. Once she was seated she looked up at O'Flynn.

"Let me introduce myself. My name is Agnes!"

Chapter Nine

Mary, Marmaduke, and Jack sat back and watched and listened as Agnes somehow, without any urging or persuasion, managed to extract O'Flynns story from him once again. It was the same as before but with a lot more detail.

When he had finished she looked at the others. "Well. He's consistent if nothing else!"

A strange look crossed O'Flynns face.

"Now why would you be saying something like that?" he asked.

Agnes held his gaze. "I'll be saying what I want young man. It seems to me that you slotted back into your old life very easily."

A look of uncertainty crossed O'Flynn's face.

Agnes continued talking. "Alexander Patrick O'Flynn wanted in Belfast, Dublin, and Liverpool. Horse theft and armed robbery mainly. You escaped to London but after a botched robbery you were caught and sentenced to death at Tyburn. The Colonel-with-no-name recruited you on the morning of your execution. Not quite as dramatic as our friend Jack here, but as a narrow an escape as you can get."

Everyone sat around the table looked at O'Flynn. He shrugged.

"To be sure life has been eventful." He raised his tankard in a toast to the others, No one moved. He gave another shrug and drank deeply.

Agnes spoke once again. "And now Mr. O'Flynn you face a difficult choice. For the past year or so you've lived the life. You've built up a sizable gang and a fearsome reputation . I dare say you have a nice little nest egg tucked away somewhere. How many robberies have you undertaken?"

She held her hand up. "No don't answer that. You achieved all you've achieved with the knowledge that somewhere hidden about your person is a special order. The same order Jack has stitched into the lining of his hat. The bit of paper that tells the reader that the possessor of the document is on Kings business, that the person is above arrest. Good insurance. No wonder you never got in touch with Jack here. You have been living a life of heads you lose, tails I win."

She leant forward. "Now My O'Flynn, tell me what choice are you going to make. Are you ready to return to your employer, the man who didn't let you hang or is the life of the Whistler too enticing? Mind you, that life could well be in jeopardy as I'm sure that as soon as Jack submits his own report the Colonel will send someone to bring you back to heel, but the choice is yours."

O'Flynn stared at Agnes. "No one knows my story. Just who the devil are you?"

Agnes smiled. "The Colonel-with-no-name knows your story and I thought I'd already introduced myself. My names Agnes."

O'Flynn looked around the table. Jack looked him in the eye and kept his face as straight as a mask. Mary held the same expression. He glanced at Marmaduke. A slight movement on the table caught his attention. He looked down to see Marmaduke's fingernails change into a set of very sharp claws. He looked back up in time to see the man smile, exposing his fangs. It put the fear of God into him.

He looked back across at Agnes. "It seems that the Whistler will be making himself scarce. In fact, from today, no one will ever hear from him again."

"The right decision!" Exclaimed Jack as he withdrew his hand from under the table. It was holding a pistol.

O'Flynn looked at him as a look of hurt spread across his face. "Bejesus Jack, had I given the wrong answer would you be after shooting me?"

"No, I would have done!" Said Mary as she placed her pistol on the table.

Agnes clapped her hands just once. "Well now we've got that settled may I suggest we focus our minds on the problem at hand. As we are sitting here an armed band of Dutch mercenaries are marching inland from the coast. They have two missions. The first is to re-establish contact with Saltersgate and the second is to eliminate The Whistler and as many of his gang as possible."

O'Flynn looked towards Agnes. "There's something else. Saltersgate are on the move. My men reported that they have sent some men to Robin Hood's Bay. I've no idea why."

Marmaduke thought out aloud. "They'll be meeting with the mercenaries. It looks like both sides are uniting to wipe you and your gang out." O'Flynn shook his head. "Maybe not. Maybe they are looking for you three and an army pay chest."

Jack sighed. "No doubt they'll try for both."

"Of course the ones we really want are the two men in the boarding house." Mary observed.

Everyone remained silent until Agnes nodded. "She's right you know. The men out on the moors are the foot soldiers. Them in the boarding house are the generals. It would be interesting to know their connections to the Dutch."

O'Flynn looked at the elderly woman. "That's fine and dandy, but it seems to me that the moors are full of men trying to kill the lot of us, how do we avoid them?"

Marmaduke gave a small growl. As he spoke O'Flynn felt the hairs on the back of his neck rise.

"We don't!" Marmaduke said.

Jack smiled and looked across at O'Flynn. "Like I said, a man of few words!"

Marmaduke ignored the comment and addressed O'Flynn. "How many men do you have out there?" O'Flynn shrugged and began counting on his fingers. "I started off with a dozen. Thanks to you that numbers down to ten."

Jack looked at him "Is that all?"

O'Flynn shook his head. "I've another dozen on the far side of the moor, but it will take half a day on a fast horse to get word to them. Then a full day for them to get here."

He looked at the faces around the table. "We don't have fast horses." He explained.

Marmaduke turned to Agnes "How many mercenaries are there?"

Agnes closed her eyes and conjured up a vision of the sight she had seen. "Twenty. Maybe a couple or three more."

Marmaduke then turned to O'Flynn. "How many will they send from Saltersgate?"

O'Flynn shook his head. "I've no idea. Maybe ten, maybe twenty."

"Don't forget those that escaped from the boarding house!" Mary added.

"Another half dozen perhaps." Marmaduke said to Agnes.

Agnes nodded.

"That's over fifty. We're outnumbered almost five to one!" O'Flynn said.

Jack smiled. "It seems a bit unfair really. They won't know what hit them!"

O'Flynn just shook his head.

Agnes picked up her tankard to take a drink and was surprised to find it empty. She put it down again.

"We need to get to the mercenaries before they meet with the Saltersgate lot." She said.

She was interrupted by an urgent knocking on the door. O'Flynn gave a snort of exasperation, stood up and strode across the floor. As he opened the door they couldn't see who was at the other side but heard a whispered conversation. O'Flynn shut the door and turned back into the room.

"We're too late. My man tells me the two groups met on the top of the moor. They are coming this way. Probably arrive here within the hour."

"Better get busy then!" remarked Agnes.

Chapter Ten

It took the best part of forty-five minutes for them to prepare themselves. Along with O'Flynn's men, who ran behind, they rode to a crossroads just outside of the village of Fylingthorpe. It lay in a depression of the moorland and was surrounded by a number of small hills.

Jack pointed out a number of positions and O'Flynn instructed his men to run across the moor to take them up.

"Keep well down until its time." He ordered their retreating backs. Soon they were invisible among the heather and undulating landscape.

Mary looked at O'Flynn, O'Flynn looked at Jack, Jack looked at Marmaduke. He looked at Agnes. She gave a slight nod and the four of them moved their horses into the centre of the crossroads.

Around her the air shimmered and Agnes simply wasn't there anymore. O'Flynn blinked and looked around. In the distance, on top of the moor, silhouetted against the sky, was the figure of an elderly woman walking across the moor. It looked like she was collecting bunches of heather. He turned to look at Jack and raised an eyebrow. Jack just shook his head.

They heard the approaching men before they came into vision. Then they crested the hill and began walking down towards the crossroads. Marmaduke counted them. There were forty or so. Some were armed with pistols, other with swords and daggers. Some carried clubs. He was looking at a small army.

As the leading group approached the crossroads they slowed down and drew their pistols aiming them at the four riders strung across the road in front of them. They were considering what to do next when a slight mist began seeping up from the heather. Within seconds the mist turned into a thick fog. Visibility was nil.

The leaders of the mercenaries turned their horses thinking to retreat to higher ground but the men behind them didn't see and for a few confused minutes riders and marching men stumbled and bumped into each other.

O'Flynn whistled his password and his men rose out of the heather and ran into the mist. The mercenary riders tried to steady their horses but all around them were noises and shouts and bumps and thumps and yells. They tried to shout out orders but such was the confusion that they went unheeded or unheard. Then after a few minutes, the mists simply dissolved away.

As their vision cleared the leaders of the mercenaries looked back along the road they had just travelled with forty or so armed men. They blinked in shock trying to work out what had happened. The road in front of them was empty. They looked behind them. The four mounted riders they had seen were still there, in the same position. They had their pistols aimed right at them. They did the only thing they could do, they dropped their weapons and raised their arms.

O'Flynn smiled and lifted a hand to his mouth, placed his fingers on either side of his lips and let go the first few notes of his tune. As it echoed through the little valley his men appeared from behind heather tussocks and out of small depressions in the ground. As they stood they bent down and dragged others onto their feet. The invaders. Some were injured, some were unconscious, all of them were firmly tied up.

The next ten minutes or so was spent persuading the captured men to line up. They were tied securely to each other, placed in some sort of order and force marched back across the moors, towards the sea and the small cove where their boats lay on the shingle.

"Won't they have left someone behind to guard the boats?" Mary asked.

"They have!" replied Agnes. She turned to Jack.

"But it's nothing you four cannot handle!"

Marmaduke turned to O'Flynn. "Can your men be trusted to march this lot back to the boat whilst we go on ahead."

O'Flynn smiled. "There's reward money to be had, beats fighting any day of the week My men won't let go of them until they've got coin in their hands."

He looked across the road to where Agnes was speaking with Mary. "Anyway, they have Agnes to keep an eye on them." He added.

He shouted an order to his men, gave his horse a slap and was off down the road. Marmaduke Jack and Mary flowed on behind.

Within thirty minutes they had reached the edge of the cliff. They dismounted and looked down into the cove where the mercenaries ships had landed. The sea was at low tide, and pulled up onto the shingle strand were two large and very sturdy boats fitted out with oars and short squat square sails. Jack nudged Marmaduke and pointed further up the beach. He followed the finger to see a small encampment higher up the beach, almost under the cliff itself. A small fire blazed around which five men lay sprawled on the sand. From the distance, it looked as if they were playing some sort of dice game. May nodded to a point further up the beach where two other men were standing at the end of a small track that led up the cliff towards them.

Marmaduke turned to Jack. "I'll take them. You look after the ones at the foot of the cliff!"

Jack nodded. O'Flynn was about to say something but Jack shook his head. "Watch and learn!" he said.

The four of them crept to the edge of the cliff until they were directly above the encampment where the men were playing their game. They scrabbled around collecting stones and large clods of earth. When they were satisfied that they had enough Marmaduke nodded and slipped away.

O'Flynn blinked against the sunlight as he watched the figure. It seemed to blur and he shook his head trying to clear his vision but all he could make out was a vague black, cat-like shape racing silently down the cliff path. He didn't see what happened next as Mary nudged him. He turned and helped the other two push the collection of rocks over the cliff edge.

There was a crash as the stones bounced down the cliff taking other rocks and loose soil with them. In a matter of seconds they were standing above a rockfall. The men at the bottom hardly had time to react when they were hit by the falling rocks and loose earth.

As O'Flynn rose to his feet to follow Jack and Mary who were already running down the cliff path he looked ahead. Marmaduke was standing where the path met the beach. At his feet two men were laying and rolling on the sand. They were both holding their faces. Before he could work out what had happened he found himself running after Jack and Mary who were now busy at the foot of the cliff extricating the injured men from the pile of rocks, earth and rubble that had covered them.

A little over an hour later a whistle from the top of the cliff informed O'Flynn that his men had arrived with the prisoners. O'Flynn gave a wave and the men began pushing and shoving their captive down the cliff path. It took another hour for them to load all the captured men onto the two boats, both the whole and the injured.

"What about them from Saltersgate?" Asked Mary.

"Let them enjoy a little cruise!" Agnes replied as a slight grin flickered over her face.

O'Flynn glanced in her direction. "You're not very nice are you?" he commented.

Agnes smiled back. "Oh, I'm very nice. Very nice indeed. That's why they are still alive!"

O'Flynn looked away and gave a little shudder.

Eventually, all the men were loaded onto the boats. They were so cramped that many of them, mostly the ones from Saltersgate, had to lay in the bottom of the boats, in the scuppers constantly being soaked by the seawater that splashed onto them.

Marmaduke and Jack moved between the as they raised the mast and the sails.

"How are they going to row with their arms tied behind them?" Mary asked.

Agnes moved her arms and a slight wind sprang up. It caught in the sails and the boats began to drift out to sea.

"By the time they've freed each other, they'll be well on their way. That wind will push them out within range of the ship waiting out there. They'll be picked up."

Agnes lowered her arms and turned to the others. "Right let's pay a visit to the lodging house. I have a feeling they might have some rooms free for the night!"

She turned to O'Flynn. "If you would be so kind as to ask your men to return to the inn at Fylingthorpe and wait for us there. Tell them not to get too drunk, we'll all be needing clear heads in the morning!"

It was growing dark as the riders arrived in Robin Hood's Bay, dismounted and tied their horses up in the small square outside the boarding house. A small stable was just up the street and Jack went to arrange stabling, leaving the horses in the hands of an ostler who led them away.

As they walked up to the door of the house they glanced behind them, across the slipway. Men were still labouring away repairing the broken stonework. Three men were standing watching. Leaning on their shovels. They looked across at the newcomers.

"Hell! There's four of them now!" One of them said as he spat a well-chewed wad of tobacco in their direction.

As they neared the door Agnes appeared from the alleyway at the side of the house. She looked up at the four of them and brushed a white feather from her shoulder. O'Flynn watched open mouthed as it floated to the cobbles.

"She only does it for effect!" Said Marmaduke under his breath.

They stood to one said as Agnes knocked on the door. They didn't have to wait long before it was opened by the landlady. Before she could say anything she found herself being propelled backwards into her own house by the firm hand of Agnes.

As they reached the hallway Agnes stopped. "We know who you are, and we know what you are doing. What you don't know is that the little army orchestrated by your two guests is heading back the way they came from. With a bit of luck, they'll be picked up tonight, or tomorrow. Now, why don't you introduce me to your guests and we....?"

Before she finished her sentence there was a movement from the doorway in front of them. A hand appeared holding a pistol. Behind her another pistol was discharged, The explosion made them all wince. There was a groan and the hand at the door dropped the pistol and retreated behind the door dripping blood.

"Very foolish!" remarked Agnes.

As she spoke, with one bound, Marmaduke had crossed the hall and kicked open the door. Behind it was a man holding a damaged hand. A pistol lay at his feet. Behind him, a second man was standing. He held his hands up.

"I am not armed!" he said.

Mary pointed her pistol at the centre of his chest.

"I'd like to make sure!" she said and walked across the room.

The man remained where he was as she felt inside his jacket and along his belt and his legs. Satisfied he was telling the truth she took a step back and nodded towards the easy chair he had just vacated. "Sit!" She demanded.

The man sat.

Agnes led the rest of the party into the room and indicated that the landlady should also sit. She indicated a second chair, well away from the other seated man.

O'Flynn held the injured man whilst Jack frisked him for weapons. He found a second pistol inside the man's jacket. He pulled it out, checked it and tucked it into his own belt.

"It's a good pistol. Foreign I believe. It could have

been made in Antwerp!"

Jack stepped forward and picked up the pistol the man had dropped. He lifted it up and examined it.

"A matching pair, expensive! Not your run of the mill pistol. This is a pistol only a gentleman of wealth could afford."

The injured man gave a grunt as he pulled his injured arm closer to his body.

"Better get that tied up or he'll bleed to death." Mary remarked.

From nowhere Agnes produced a white bandage and a small pot of salve. The man winced as she rubbed it onto his wound.

"It's only a flesh wound." She told him. "It's gone right through the flesh between your thumb and finger. You're lucky to have your fingers left!"

The man grunted as Agnes bound the wound up.

"This is an outrage, an intrusion! How dare you enter my house and attack my guests. I'll have you know this is a respectable...."

The landlady never had the opportunity to finish her sentence. The man in the chair made a sudden move. From down the side of the chair he was sitting in he produced a pistol. The quiet of the room was shattered by the sound of four pistols firing together.

The last thing the man in the chair saw before his chest imploded by the force of three balls hitting him in the same place at the same time, was his bullet leave his pistol, heading straight towards Agnes.

He never saw the look of fear and consternation cross everyone's face as they turned to watch the bullet and its trajectory.

Agnes blinked and moved her finger. The bullet stopped in mid-flight, about three inches from her face. She reached forward and plucked it from the frozen air. She held it towards her, looked at it, shook her head sadly and dropped it into her pocket,

"It didn't have my name on it!" She said as she finished tying the bandage. She looked at the landlady who was slumped in her chair.

"She's fainted!" Said Mary.

Agnes nodded. "Leave her be. This is the man we need to speak to."

They all turned to look at the wounded man. He looked up from the bandage.

"You'd better sit down." Agnes told him.

The man sat.

Anges turned to Jack. "I suggest that you, Mary and O'Fynn here go through this house from top to bottom. Let's see what we can find. I'll be fine here. Marmaduke will make sure of that."

Marmaduke gave a small growl. The woman in the chair remained unconscious. Agnes checked her breathing.

"She'll be fine. She'll come round in her own time. Off you go!"

Mary pointed at the chair where the dead man lay slumped. "What about him?"

Agnes looked, noting the blood that oozed out of his shattered chest forming a puddle on the floor before being absorbed and spreading a deep red stain in the carpet.

"He ain't going to come back to life. I think I'll be safe enough. No doubt someone, somewhere will want his body returned." She said as she looked at the injured man still holding his bandaged hand.

"And you can move him into the centre of the room, well away from the walls. This house is riddled with hidden passages and I wouldn't want him falling through any secret panels."

The man shuffled across the room and sat in the chair Agnes has indicated.

Jack, Mary, and O'Flynn left the room, separated and began their thorough search of the house.

Agnes picked up a chair and sat opposite the injured man. She looked into his face.

"My name is Agnes. Would you be so kind as to furnish me with your name?"

The man said nothing but looked defiantly back at her.

"Well please yourself." She looked at Marmaduke. He took a step forward and growled in the man's face.

"Dus je bedoelt om marteling. Hoe brave!" He spat out the words.

"Nee, ik wil gewoon praten!" Replied Agnes.

The man looked surprised.

"Yes," Agnes said, "I can speak Dutch. I also know that you speak perfectly good English. So let's stop playing games. Who are you?"

The man sighed and began to place his good hand inside his jacket. Marmaduke pulled back his trigger. The man looked up at him and very slowly opened the jacket. There was no concealed weapon. Instead, he pulled out a card and leant forward presenting it to Agnes. She took it and read it.

"Mr. John Pettigrew, purveyor of fine wines." She read out.

She turned the card around. It was blank. Very carefully she turned it over again and then ripped it in two and dropped the pieces on the floor.
She turned to Marmaduke. "Well, I tried the nice way!"

She looked back to the man who had returned his attention to his injured hand. She wriggled her fingers and a grey mist drifted into the room. The man looked up as it engulfed him. Within seconds the man inside the mist let out a scream. Agnes moved her finger and the mist dissolved. The man was still seated there but he had changed. He looked older and his hair was whiter. His eyes were wide open. He stared wild-eyed at Agnes. She stared back.

"Now let's start from the beginning. You arrived from a ship moored out in the North Sea. You work for the Dutch Crown or their Government. Your mission is, or rather was, to operate a network of spies. To pay for their service you trade in opium which, indirectly, is supplied by your masters and which you deliver to the Saltersgate men. They are in your pay. Everything ran smoothly until someone called the Whistler killed your agent."

She paused and looked at the man's face. His eyes were even wider open. Now he began to sweat and shiver a little. Agnes smiled.

"It's not very nice is it, having someone else inside your head. Now, just in case you think I'm pretending, you live in Antwerp, you have a daughter and a son. Your wife died two years ago and your dog's name is.... Do you want me to continue?"

The man shook his head.

Agnes continued speaking. "Now that wasn't bad was it? Hardly "*foltering*" as you would say.

The man looked up at Agnes. "The visions!" he stuttered.

Agnes looked down and brushed the front of her skirt. "Oh those! Well, when someone is confronted by their greatest fears it forces their mind to concentrate on combating the fear. That's when I slip in around the back. It's a bit like knocking on the front door and when you answer it I slip in through the back."

She looked back at Marmaduke. "You understand don't you?"

Marmaduke shrugged.

A groan caused the three of them to look at the landlady. She was emerging from her faint. Careful she looked around the room. The first thing she saw was the dead body slumped in her chair. Her hands instantly rose to her face.

"Not pretty is it? Perhaps you had better get a sheet and cover him up."

There was a sudden crash from upstairs. The landlady looked anxiously towards the ceiling.

Agnes looked across to her. "Sorry about that. My companions can be a little clumsy. Of course, you could tell us what they could find and where they will find it."

The woman remained tight-lipped and stared angrily at Agnes. Agnes stared right back at her. Within thirty seconds the woman looked away. The man in the chair said something in Dutch. Agnes .looked at him.

"In English please!" She returned her gaze to the landlady.

"He told you that the games up. You have been discovered."

A look of surprise crossed the woman's face. Agnes continued. "Oh that's just a rough translation, but he's right. I'm afraid your enterprise has come to an end."

Once again the woman glanced at the dead man and she seemed to shrink. Her hands went up to her face and she leant over and started to cry.

There was a noise at the door. They looked up to see Jack and O'Flynn standing there. O'Flynn held two muskets, Jack held a brace of pistols.

"In the attic!" He said.

"Anything else?" Agnes asked.

"Just this!"

They turned to see Mary walk down the corridor. She was hauling a large waterproof sack that she dragged into the room.

"Don't bother helping!" She said as she pushed Jack out of the way. Marmaduke moved forward and helped her pull it into the room.

"Ever the gentleman!" remarked O'Flynn.

Marmaduke gave him a stare. "I live with Agnes!" he said.

O'Flynn glanced at Agnes, She was sitting there watching the exchange.

O'Flynn reddened "I see what you mean!" he murmured.

Mary reached into the sack and pulled out a small well-sealed package.

"Just like the ones the donkey man was carrying." Agnes observed.

As she spoke Mary pulled out a dagger and cut off the wrapping.

"Opium?" asked Jack.

Mary scratched at the contents with her fingernail and sniffed. She nodded. "I think so. I've never seen it before."

From her seat across the room, Agnes sniffed the air.

"Opium!" she confirmed.

"Now what?" asked Marmaduke.

O'Flynn looked up at Jack. "I see what you mean. Straight to the point!"

Agnes stood up. "Lock these two in a bedroom, preferably one with small windows and we'll make some decisions."

After the landlady and the injured Dutchman had been locked in a small bedroom, and after Agnes had cast a sealing spell over the door, the windows, the locked door and for good measure, the fireplace and the chimney, the four of the gathered in the kitchen of the house.

From nowhere four cups of tea appeared. O'Flynn looked at his cup with suspicion. Agnes looked over the edge of her cup at him. "This is what we'll do."

As she spoke the rest of them made themselves as comfortable as the kitchen furniture could allow. Mary sat on the large wooden table. Jack leant against a dresser. O'Flynn and Marmaduke sat on two chairs whilst Agnes stood with her back to the fire. It was burning low. She moved a finger and it flared up again. She turned back towards the rest of the room.

"I am going to contact the Colonel-with-no-name!"

O'Flynn looked up at her. "Now that will be a fine trick!"

Jack turned to him. "It is!" he said.

O'Flynn shut up.

Agnes ignored both of them. "I'll also contact the Commander at Scarborough Garrison. No doubt the army will want to take charge of our spies. It might take some discretion, there might be diplomatic problems."

Jack finished his tea and looked around for somewhere to put his cup. "The last I heard we were at war with the Dutch. How much more of a diplomatic incident can there be?"

Agnes gave him a look as she continued. "Also it will take the army to get wagons and transport, collect the opium and the payroll and escort it safely back to the Garrison."

She looked across at O'Flynn. "Just removing temptation!" she remarked.

O'Flynn nodded.

"Whilst I do that I suggest you four better get some rest. I'm assuming you'll be riding at first light."

Mary glanced at Marmaduke, Marmaduke looked at O'Flynn and O'Flynn looked at Jack. Jack looked at Agnes and raised an eyebrow.

"Saltersgate?" he asked.

"Saltersgate." She agreed.

Chapter Eleven

As the rest slept Agnes silently closed the kitchen door behind her. She moved her hand across the entrance and took a step into the yard. The air shimmered and a seagull rose in the air. It hovered above the red roofs before turning and flying down the coast. It followed the breakers, shining white in the moonlight until it came to the familiar skyline of Scarborough and the Castle.

The Commander was sat in his private quarters. A warming pan was heating his bed and he had undone the buttons down the front of his tunic. A large tumbler of whiskey was at his side. In one hand he held a large ornate mirror, in the other a pair of small scissors. He peered into the glass and brought the scissors up to the end of his moustache. Just as he was about to make a cut the air behind him shimmered and an elderly lady was standing behind him. He jumped in surprise and turned. As he turned he snipped one end off his moustache.

"Good grief woman! What are you thinking of? These are my private rooms."

The red mist dropped from his eyes as he realised who was standing in front of him.

"Oh! It's you!" he stuttered.

"Well, I've had better welcomes!" Agnes said. As she spoke she brushed her shoulder. A large white feather fluttered down towards the floor. The Commander blinked.

Agnes walked across the room and .looked at the Commander's glass. "You'd better top it up. I have a long story to tell."

As Agnes related the story of the Whistler and the

events and discovery's at Robin Hood's Bay the Commander took sip after sip from his tumbler until he realised his glass was empty. Agnes reached over and filled it up for him as she continued her tale. When she had finished the Commander blinked once more.

"Good grief Agnes. Arriving in a gentleman's room in the middle of the night is a bit off hand."

He gave a cough and realised his jacket was undone. He began to button up. Agnes coughed politely and gave him one of her looks.

"Commander, with the greatest respect. If I wanted to visit you in your private room in the middle of the night, dressed or undressed, I would have done so by now. However as I find myself in the possession of a large quantity of opium and a chest full of army gold, not to mention two Dutch spies, well I'm sure under the circumstances you'll excuse my lack of a calling card."

The Commander spluttered and let out a harrumph and reached for his tumbler. It was empty. He refilled it again. He took a sip and let lose another harrumph.

"Bit of a shock, don't you know. Chap doesn't expect visitations in his own rooms." He pulled at the front of his tunic. "Suppose you want something done."

He tried to rise and realised he had stood too quickly in relation to the amount of whiskey he'd consumed. He put his hands on the arms of his chair to steady himself.

"Despatch a couple of dozen troopers at first light?" he suggested.

Agnes nodded. "Better send a couple of wagons as well." She added.

"Better organise it now." The Commander said as

he tottered unsteadily across the room. He opened his door and bellowed down the corridor.

"Get Lieutenant Smalls. I don't care if he's abed. I don't care where he is. Get him here now!"

He turned back to Agnes. "Where's this place again?"

Agnes explained the position of the boarding house, and then found she had to explain where Robin Hood's Bay was. Just to make sure she drew the Commander a small sketch map in the air in front of her.

There was the noise of running feet coming along the corridor and the Commander opened the door and stuck his head out into the corridor.

"Lieutenant Smalls! Emergency. We need to muster the troops!"

He turned back into his room. It was empty. He looked around. In the middle of the floor was a piece of paper. He looked down. It was a sketch map of Robin Hood's Bay. On top of it lay a white seagull feather.

As the Lieutenant entered the room the Commander realised the window was open. The Lieutenant looked around the room and understood the scene in one glance.

"Agnes?" He asked.

The Commander nodded and reached out for his decanter leaving the Lieutenant to wonder what had occurred to make the Commander cut off the end of his moustache.

It was a couple of hours before dawn as Agnes walked back to the kitchen of the boarding house to find Marmaduke sat back with his boots up on the cast iron oven set aside the fire grate. The fire was smouldering. He leant forward and placed some coal on the embers. A brownish smoke rose.

"Sea coal!" remarked Agnes.

Marmaduke turned to her. "The Commander will help?"

Agnes smiled. "Lieutenant Smalls has been ordered to lead a platoon of troopers here complete with a couple of wagons. They'll be leaving at first light."

Marmaduke nodded. He looked serious. "I hope they come prepared!"

Agnes raised an eyebrow. "Why do you say that?"

Marmaduke scratched at his whiskers. "Well, it's just that a shipment of opium side by side with an army payroll chest is a big temptation."

Agnes sat down and looked at Marmaduke. "There's only us and the Commander know what they will be escorting!"

Marmaduke nodded. "I know that!"

Agnes moved her hands and two cups of tea appeared on the table behind them. She waited as Marmaduke took a sip.

"Go on then. What are you worried about?"

Marmaduke carefully poured his tea into the saucer and began lapping at the drink. Agnes said nothing but waited patiently until he replaced the saucer onto the table.

He looked at Agnes. "I have my doubts about O'Flynn."

Agnes raised her other eyebrow. Marmaduke

continued. "He's had two years out here on the moor, he's established himself!"

"He's undercover!" Agnes replied.

Marmaduke paused for a second. "Too deeply undercover for my liking."

He turned and looked into her face. "It's a big temptation. The army payroll and the opium would make him rich for the rest of his days!"

Agnes leant back in her chair. "You think he will try to double-cross us?"

Marmaduke shrugged. "He could be leading us straight into a trap. Perhaps the Saltersgate lot have joined up with his gang. Perhaps they are waiting for us at Fylingthorpe where they can ambush us."

Agnes remained silent as she thought this over. Eventually, she turned to Marmaduke."Surely if he was planning to do anything he wouldn't have allowed some of the Saltersgate men to be captured yesterday."

Marmaduke stopped scratching. "That was before we found the opium and you decided to send the payroll back."

Agnes nodded. "In which case, I suggest you leave for Saltersgate later in the morning. If he is planning something it will be hard to lead us into an ambush at Saltersgate and attack the army on their way back to the Garrison."

Marmaduke shrugged. "We'll see!" He said.

The night passed uneventfully and, as the rooms in the boarding house proved extremely comfortable, everyone had a deep and refreshing sleep. As the dawn broke it found Agnes up and about cooking up a breakfast of eggs and ham that she had found in the larder. Her scrying bowl lay on the edge of the table.

Marmaduke appeared and sat in an easy chair and began to clean his pistol. Jack was the next to arrive.

"Shouldn't we be on our way?" he asked.

Marmaduke shrugged. "Change of plan. We're leaving later in the morning."
Jack looked at him an unspoken question on his lips.

"Insurance!" Marmaduke simply said.

Jack had demolished a plateful of eggs and ham as the door to the kitchen opened and O'Flynn stood there.

"I was worried I'd missed you. I slept in. You can say what you like about our Dutch friends but they know how to keep comfortable rooms."

He looked around. "You seem to be taking your time." He said as Jack helped himself to another slice of ham.

"There's no rush!" Marmaduke said. "We're leaving later in the morning."

A quick look appeared and disappeared across O'Flynn's face before he forced a smile and sat down at the table.

"In which case, I think I can do justice to that ham sitting there." He said helping himself to breakfast.

The same conversation was held a few minutes later when Mary appeared already dressed for the road. She said nothing but gave Jack a quick glance. Jack just shook his head slightly. After they had eaten O'Flynn pushed himself away from the table and stood up.

"I think I'll just check on the horses. Make sure

they are still where we left them."

Everybody watched as he stood up and looked out of the back door. After the door had been shut for a couple of minutes Jack turned to Marmaduke.

"Now, what's really going on?"

Marmaduke turned to look at him and placed a finger on his lips. Quickly he rose to his feet and moved across to the small window by the side of the door. He looked outside. The back yard was deserted, there was no sign of O'Flynn. He turned back to the room.

"How much do you estimate the payroll and the opium is worth?"

Jack scratched his head, unable to come up with an answer.

"A lot!" suggested Mary.

"Enough to tempt our friend to return to his Whistler identity?" Marmaduke asked them.

They said nothing but an anxious look was exchanged between them.

Marmaduke stretched. "I'm not saying he will. I'm just saying it's a possibility. If you count up his men and add those up at Saltersgate it amounts to quite a number. Enough to ambush a troop of soldiers up on the moors."

Jack was doing some quick thinking. Slowly he nodded his head.

"I think O'Flynn is an opportunist. He's like a small tree, bends with the wind. I find it difficult to believe he never had an opportunity to get word to me in the last two years."

"So what do you think he'll do now?" Asked Mary.

"I think if there's no opportunity to steal the money or the opium he'll stay with us. However, if such a chance does present itself, well who knows!" Marmaduke replied.

The door to the back room opened and Agnes walked into the kitchen. As she closed the door behind her she brushed a white feather from her shoulder. Marmaduke let out a short groan. Jack exchanged a look with Mary.

"Busy out there!" Agnes said.

The rest remained quiet, she carried on.

"The army troops are about a mile away. Goodness knows what time they left the Garrison. O'Flynn's men are gathering at Fylingthorpe. There seems to be more of them than there were yesterday."

The three people sat at the table exchanged a look.

Agnes continued. "Oh yes, and our friend did check the horses. Whilst he was there he had a chat with someone who seemed to be waiting for him. After they had finished I watched him. He headed out of the Bay and towards Fylingthorpe."

"Hell's teeth! The man's taking us for fools!" Exclaimed Jack.

Agnes shook her head. "No not fools. Personally, I don't think that the man has made his mind up. At the moment he's running with the hare and the hounds. He'll finally decide when the time's right. Just make sure you watch your backs!"

The three of them sighed, then Agnes added, "Mind you if you take the army with you it might even up the odds a bit!"

There was a hurried discussion. They agreed. They would wait for the army to arrive and lead them to Flyingthorpe and onto Saltersgate. O'Flynn returned to the house and joined Marmaduke, Mary and Jack outside in watching the labourers still hard at work repairing the slipway.

It was a full two hours before the Army arrived. Agnes wasn't that surprised to see the garrison Commander at its head followed by Lieutenant Smalls. The Commander set up his headquarters in the kitchen whilst Lieutenant Smalls supervised the transfer of the opium to the wagon parked outside the house. Whilst they were alone Agnes took the opportunity of explaining their reservations about O'Flynn.

The Commander harrumphed. "Better keep a weather eye on the bounder!" he said.

Outside, their curiosity aroused, the workmen stopped their labour, leant on their shovels and watched the army. As the packages were transferred the troopers ringed the area outside the house and a crowd began to gather. Anyone who ventured too near was met by a trooper with a loaded musket. All questions remained unanswered. Rumours flew but the sight of the muskets was enough to keep even the most curious away.

Once the contraband had been stored in the wagon Agnes and Marmaduke went upstairs and brought down the two prisoners. It seemed as if the pair were sleepwalking as they were led to the rear of the cart, helped up, bedded down on blankets and returned to a deep sleep. Then the strange party left Robin Hood's Bay, they travelled up the town by the main road and then took the moorland road heading towards Fylingthorpe.

The Lieutenant had arranged the order of the troops. He led at the front with half a dozen troopers forming a phalanx. Next came the two carts, steered by troopers with muskets close by their sides. Four other troopers rode either side of the carts. Behind them was a second phalanx of troopers closely followed by five riders. The Commander rode alongside Marmaduke, Jack, Mary, and O'Flynn. Everyone rode at full alert their eyes flashing right to left. High above them, a seagull circled in the sky.

They had travelled a couple of miles along the moorland road when a figure appeared at the side of the road. It was Agnes. She was sat on a black wooden box.

"I believe this belongs to you!" she said to the Lieutenant.

No one bothered to ask how or where or anything else for that matter. They just loaded the chest containing the payroll onto the second wagon and continued on their way. Above them a seagull circled.

The ambush happened a few miles away. The party had followed the road and arrived where a depression in the moor led the route into a large dip. As the lead troops were in the deepest part of the dip men appeared on the skyline above them. They were spotted by Lieutenant Smalls at the head of the troop, who quickly turned his horse and barked out a series of orders. Within seconds the troops had formed a circle around the wagons. Each man pointed his musket at the top of the hill. At the rear of the circle, Marmaduke leapt from his horse and half ran and half bounded up the hill keeping low. Jack and Mary drew their pistols. O'Flynn sat on his horse scanning the horizon. Jack turned towards him.

"Time to make your mind up O'Flynn! Either join your men or stand with us!"

O'Flynn looked from the horizon towards Jack. He noticed the pistol pointed directly at his chest.

"Now why would I be a wanting to go and do a thing like that?" he asked.

Jack nodded towards the wagon. "I can think of a few reasons!"

Before O'Flynn could answer a volley of shots were fired from the top of the hill. Balls whizzed around them, some of them embedded themselves into the carts and a trooper fell backwards from his horse.

"Fire!"

The command had been shouted by the Lieutenant. A second volley of shots echoed across the moor. Despite the troopers being outnumbered their better weapons and accuracy made up for the difference. On either side of them, on the skyline men fell, only to be replaced by others. The Commander climbed up onto the rear of one of the carts and began to load a musket.

There was a movement on the road behind them. A group of the attackers had crept over the heather and were attempting to charge the party from the rear. Mary noticed them first and discharged both her pistols. One man fell clutching his chest. Without thinking Jack turned his horse, dug his spurs in and drawing his sword charged at them. Seeing what was happening the troopers nearest him gave covering fire. From the back of the cart, the Commander barked out an order.

"For God's sake, go after him!"

Two troopers immediately charged after Jack, drawing their own sabres.

The three of them hit the oncoming men like a ball hitting a set of skittles. Those that were not sent sprawling by the horses were cut down by the sabres flashing in the sunlight. The ones who remained standing turned and took to their heels running back up onto the moor.

More gunfire echoed around the valley. This time the fire had been concentrated on the front of the troop. One musket ball skimmed across the shoulder of the Lieutenant ripping his epaulet and causing a scorch mark along the side of his neck. The trooper next to him wasn't so lucky.

"For God's sake take cover!" Shouted the Commander as he and the driver leapt down from their exposed position. The driver of the second cart followed suit. They took up positions by the side of the carts.

At the rear, Jack and the two troopers returned at the gallop. As they pulled their horses to a halt Jack saw Mary sitting on her horse. She was looking down reloading one of her pistols as another volley of shots peppered the air around them. Realising she was exposed she leapt off her horse and took shelter behind the cart. Above her, O'Flynn was still sitting astride his horse. Jack shouted for him to get down when O'Flynn lifted his hand to his chest, turned and looked at him. Jack noticed that a large patch of red was spreading across the man's tunic. As the troopers around him fired their muskets Jack made a flying dismount and landed on the ground just in time to catch O'Flynn as he fell backwards from his horse. Ignoring the musket balls as they hit and bounced off the road around him Jack dragged O'Flynn under the cart. Mary looked across at him. Jack merely shrugged and looked around him. They were already outnumbered and now had four or five men down. It was only a matter of time before they were all picked off. He glanced to the second wagon where the Commander and the Lieutenant were holding a hurried conversation. As he looked his nose twitched. He could smell smoke, something was burning. He looked up at the crest of the nearest hill. The heather was on fire. He looked around, The fire had spread unnoticed and seemed to form a circle all around them. The strange thing about it was that the fire wasn't travelling down the hill. It was burning upwards, away from the troopers and the carts. Now the crest of the hill was covered in a thick black smoke. Flames could be seen leaping into the sky.

This was the opportunity Marmaduke had been waiting for. Under cover of the smoke his body twitched and changed shape. In seconds a large black cat bounded off into the smoke. The creature came across the first group of attackers as they stood up coughing and spluttering as the smoke engulfed them. They had no idea what hit them. Suddenly they found themselves in the centre of a very violent black hurricane that seemed to rip and tear at their faces and bodies. It was all over in seconds. Of the seven men who had stood up, not one remained upright. Instead, as the smoke rose, they lay in a bloody mass, holding deeply scratched and torn arms and legs. One had been clawed across his face, the deep scratches revealing his teeth and jaw bone. Another had suffered his throat being ripped open. He lay in the heather choking on his own blood.

Marmaduke hit a second group of men just as violently, viciously and just as deadly. Satisfied that the men no longer presented a threat Marmaduke turned and bounded back down the hill. As he emerged from the smoke his body twitched.

Mary looked up as Marmaduke loped back towards the cart. His face and clothing were blackened by the smoke and fire, but it was his hands that caught her attention. They were dripping with blood. She gave a slight shiver.

"Let me look at O'Flynn!"

The sudden voice behind her made her jump. She turned to see Agnes standing next to Jack. He nodded towards the cart. Before she got down on her hands and knees Agnes turned to the Commander.

"Tell your men to make a charge straight up the

road ahead. Once they are through the smoke they will find around twenty or so men. They are in the process of re-grouping, you'll catch them unawares. Oh yes, and another thing, about half a dozen riders are heading across the moor as fast as they can. I think they are heading towards Saltersgate."

With that, she squatted down and crawled under the cart. She looked down at O'Flynns face. He was still alive. He opened his eyes and looked back at her.

"Not too sure that magic can help!" he stuttered.

Agnes said nothing but rummaged in her pocket and pulled out a pair of scissors and began cutting away at his clothing.

"Don't you go wasting time on me!" O'Flynn murmured.

"Just for once shut up O'Flynn!" Agnes said as she put her hand onto his wound. The bleeding stopped. She looked into his face.

"This will hurt!" she said.

O'Flynn gritted his teeth. His body jerked and his head fell back. He let out a slight groan. Then he opened his eyes once more. Agnes was holding something in her hand. It was a musket ball.

"You can have it as a reminder. You can wonder whether it came from a Saltersgate musket or from a member of the Whistlers gang. The bleedings stopped but I need to put some salve on the wound. It will stop the infection. Now go to sleep. You can check whether it had your name on it later."

As O'Flynn's eyes closed she slipped the ball into his jacket pocket and crawled out from under the cart. As she stood up she looked around her. Marmaduke was standing next to her.

"Where's everyone gone?" she asked.

Marmaduke pointed up the road towards the smoke.

"They've all gone?" she asked.

"Apart from the troopers who are injured. Nothing serious too serious but the Commander thought they'd be better deployed looking after us."

Agnes looked across to where some troopers were laid on their stomachs pointing their muskets at the smoke where it met the road. She nodded.

"Jack and Mary went with them?"

"Of course!" replied Marmaduke.

"Has anyone checked on the two prisoners? She asked

Marmaduke shrugged. "I'd forgotten all about them."

Agnes climbed up onto one of the wagons and looked in the back of the cart. Two figures lay side by side, wrapped up in blankets. They were fast asleep and unscathed. She climbed back down and noticed a trooper with a tourniquet around his thigh.

"Let me have a look at that lad!" She said.

She had just finished treating the last trooper who had received a severe graze along the side of his face from a musket ball and had just finished telling him how lucky he was when she heard the sound of horses coming back down the road. She turned to see the Commander and his Lieutenant leading their troops out of the smoke.

"Came out of the smoke at them like a bunch of

whirling Dervishes." The Commander shouted across to her.

"Anybody hurt?" She asked.

The Lieutenant shook his head. "A lot of their side fell or fled. None of our lads received as much as a scratch. We hit them before they realised we were on them."

He looked down at Agnes. "Funny that. We took them totally by surprise. They never even heard our horses."

"It must have been the smoke." Replied Agnes, holding his look. "It must have been so dense as to muffle the sound!"

The Lieutenant shook his head. "When we came out of the smoke we still had fifty yards to gallop and they still didn't seem to hear us!"

Agnes gave a shrug. "As you say, funny that!"

Jack and Mary returned just as the smoke began to dissipate and all traces of the fire disappeared.

"What's left of them are heading back across the moor. Saltersgate I would imagine." Jack shouted down to them.

"Well, we'd better be off after them!" Agnes replied.

The Commander harrumphed. "Just a minute there. We've beaten them. All they can do is to lick their wounds. I'm in charge of two carts containing an army payroll and more contraband than I can shake a stick at. The last thing I intend doing is to charge a nest of vipers holding such a valuable cargo. Good God it would be like charging a thirsty man with barrels of water!"

Marmaduke furrowed his brow. He wasn't sure

what the Commander meant, but he knew that the man didn't think much of Agnes's idea! As the thought crossed his mind there seemed to be a flash and a sparkle in the air around them.

"What carts?" Agnes asked the Commander.

Everyone looked behind them. The two carts simply weren't there. All that remained was the sleeping form of O'Flynn, the wounded troopers, and some grasses bent over where the cart wheels had stood.

The Commander turned red in the face. "My God, how am I going to explain that in reports?" he exploded.

The Lieutenant just looked up into the sky. Mary sat on her horse with her mouth wide open. Jack just laughed.

"Well that was easy!" he said.

Agnes gave him one of those looks. "If you knew just how not easy disappearing two carts, complete with occupants and contraband is, you wouldn't even think that!"

Jack stopped laughing.

Agnes turned to the Commander. "Well, what are you waiting for? Get after them. Attack now and you'll get the entire wasps nest. I'll stay here and keep an eye on the injured."

She turned to Jack. "At least you have a chance to get in there."

Jack shook his head. "There will be nothing left by the time this lot have attacked. Anything incriminating will be destroyed at the first attack."

Agnes smiled at him. "Look underneath the fireplace!" She said.

Chapter Twelve

The outlaws, bandits, and robbers that made up the combined force of the men from Whistlers old gang and the men from Saltersgate Made quick time across the moors. Marmaduke, Jack, Mary and the troopers followed at full gallop.

"No point in allowing them to get bedded in!" The Lieutenant shouted to his men.

Jack turned in his saddle. "They'll already be prepared. Some men left earlier." He shouted back.

The company drew to a halt at the crest of a hill above the Saltersgate Inn. The view that spread out below then was spectacular. In the distance, they could see the moor stretching away to the horizon. Distant hills and woods could be made out in the late afternoon sun. Directly below them, a road dissected the landscape. It was the main Whitby to Pickering road. The inn nestled in a corner where the road rose up a hill before taking a sharp turn to the left. All around the inn men were dismounting and running into the building. Some took positions up at the rear of the building. As the last man entered the inn the door was shut and the windows shuttered. Guns and musket barrels appeared poking out of any gaps. Jack pointed to the side of the house. At the top just under the chimney stack was a window.

"Armed lookouts." He said.

The Commander turned to his Lieutenant. "Who's the best sharpshooters we have?" he asked.

The Lieutenant turned and shouted out three names and three troopers urged their horses forward.

"Concentrate on that window. In your own time!" he told them

The men dismounted and carefully took their long-barrelled guns from their saddles. Each one knelt down on one knee and steadied their aim.

"Fire at will!" The Commander shouted.

The three muskets cracked as one and in the distance the window shattered. Glass and wooden splinters fell to the ground. A second volley rang out and the stones around the windows cracked and flaked away sending sharp shards spinning to the ground.

The shots were returned from someone in an upstairs window, but the troopers were just out of range.

"Now what?" Asked Mary.

"I have an idea!" replied Jack.

He leant across to Marmaduke and whispered

something in his ear. Marmaduke listened and then nodded. Jack put a hand inside his jacket and drew something out that he handed to Marmaduke as the man slid from his horse and disappeared into the landscape.

Jack turned to the Commander. "Sir, may I suggest that you ready your troops for a downhill charge."

The Commander looked at the inn and then at Jack. "Are you mad Sir? A frontal attack would be a disaster. Out of the question!"

"As soon as you see the explosion charge." Jack said.

"What explosion?" The Commander asked feeling annoyed as his words seem to have been ignored. Meanwhile, the Lieutenant had been watching Marmaduke. The man had dismounted and run to the edge of the hill, as he moved the air around him had seemed to shimmer. Then instead of the tall ginger, one-eared man the Lieutenant realised he was looking at a large black cat-like shape that disappeared downhill under cover of the heather.

As the Commander and Jack continued to exchange words the Lieutenant continued to watch in fascination as the shape moved almost invisibly over the heather, down the hill and moved towards the building. A flash of understanding hit him. He turned to his troops.

"Mount up!" he ordered. The troopers took to horse.

"Prepare to charge!" he shouted.

The Commander was just about to counteract the order when there was a loud explosion from the rear of the house. The company began their charge just as the windows and doors blew out from the front of the building.

The fight didn't last long. As bloodied and bruised men stumbled out from the shattered space where a door once stood they saw a platoon of troopers bearing down on them with drawn sabres. Instantly they dropped their weapons and held their hands high above their heads. The troopers pulled their mounts to a halt and aimed their weapons at the surrendering men.

Jack continued riding around the side of the building and came to the small yard at the rear. Marmaduke was standing there with two pistols drawn. Jack looked to where they were pointing. In front of Marmaduke was a large hole in the rear of the building where a door once stood. Next to the door was a shattered window, its wooden frame hanging crazily in shreds. Rubble was spread around inside and outside of the hole. In and among the rubble he could see figures. Some were not moving, others stumbled and fell among the smoke and the dust.

He drew his pistols. "If anyone can move, now is a good time to stand up and come out, preferably with your arms above your heads!"

He looked across to Marmaduke. "I told you a little bit of dynamite goes a long way!"

Marmaduke looked back at him and grinned. His fangs were showing. "It certainly saves a lot of time and effort!" he remarked and turned back to peering into the hole.

It took the best part of an hour for the troopers to go through the ruined building, searching for any men who may have thought hiding was a good idea.

Some injured men were found unconscious among the rubble, the dust, and the debris. They were carried outside where they joined the other stunned and injured men they had found and who had been led outside the inn and lined up.

Once they were sure the building was deserted the Commander turned to his Lieutenant. "I suppose we have to march these bounders back to the Castle." he harrumphed.

The Lieutenant nodded towards a group of injured men lying at the side of the road. "They can't march!" he observed.

The Commander harrumphed once again. "We need Agnes and the dashed carts!" he commented.

They looked around hoping she was standing close. She wasn't but you could never tell with Agnes. As the military men pondered their dilemma Marmaduke turned to Jack.

"Not much chance of finding and uncovering your spy network!" he remarked.

Jack looked at the line of prisoners. "One of them knows something!"

Mary laughed. "Whoever it is they won't stand up and admit it!"

Jack turned and looked at the damaged inn. "It will take them a long time to re-establish this link, if they ever bother. We have destroyed the Robin Hood's Bay connection so there's no need for this route any longer."

Marmaduke scratched the whiskers on his chin. "Didn't Agnes mention something about looking under the fireplace?"

Jack turned and ran into the building. Marmaduke and Mary exchanged a look and followed him back inside.

The inside of the bar room was almost destroyed. In the centre of what was once a room, there was a large hole in the ceiling. Timbers leant at crazy angles, smashed furniture lay among the stones and the rubble. At the far end of the building, standing in a large fireplace that seemed undamaged was a large cast iron range. Its fire was still burning. Jack ran straight to the fireplace. At first glance, it looked solid. He grabbed the edge of the range and promptly burnt his hand. He gave a yelp and pulled it back quickly, just missing Marmaduke's head who was stood behind him looking over his shoulder at the burning fire. Before either of them could say anything there was a shower of sparks and the place filled up with steam. They turned around to see Mary standing behind them with an empty bucket.

"What?" She asked. "It was only the slops that were behind what's left of the bar!"

The two men said nothing but turned back to examine the steaming range. Marmaduke bent down and looked at the ground in front of it.

"There's some sort of line here. It runs right around the edge of the fireplace."

Jack looked and began tug at the rear of the fireplace. Marmaduke rummaged in the rubble and found a broken table leg. He rammed it behind the fireplace and using it as a lever, began to pull. The fireplace moved slightly.

"Harder!" Marmaduke grunted as Jack got a grip on the wood.

Mary found a piece of broken doorway and rammed it behind the fireplace on the opposite side then she pulled at it. The fireplace gave another slight move and the crack began to show.

Mary stopped tugging and looked across to Jack. "We're not getting very far. Have you got any of that dynamite left?"

Jack shook his head. Marmaduke suddenly let go of the wooden lever, turned and leapt out of the room. He returned holding a length of rope.

"Tie this around it!" he said as he threw one end at Jack.

As he looped the rope around the back of the iron range he looked up at Marmaduke.

"What's on the other end?" he asked.

"The troopers horses!" Marmaduke replied.

Mary leant out of the shattered window. Outside she saw a long line of prisoners roped and fastened together. Two carts had appeared on the side of the road. As she looked up she realised that Agnes was sat in the driving seat of one of them. As she saw the surprise on Mary's face Agnes gave her a cheery wave. Mary watched as Agnes hopped down and walked over to where the wounded lay. In seconds she was on her knees tending to the more seriously injured. She also noticed there was a small line of bodies covered by old bits of sacking. They were the ones who had either perished by the explosion or had been cut down by the troopers. She shook her head. She looked at where the door once was and saw that the rope was now stretched taught and was being pulled by six of the horses that a trooper had roped together.

She turned back into the room and looked at the fireplace. As the tension in the rope increased and the horses strained as they stepped forward there was a crash and the iron grate was ripped from its position in the fireplace. A second crash sounded as it fell over and spilt wet coals and ashes across the floor. Where it stood was a hole in the floor. The range had been dragged halfway across the room when it became stuck in the debris. Marmaduke gave a shout and the tension in the rope slackened. He turned around to see Jack and Mary looking down into the hole, he walked across and took a look himself.

"Found something have you?" A voice said.

They turned around to see the Commander closely followed by the Lieutenant picking their way towards them through the rubble and the debris.

"We need a lantern!" Said Mary.

They searched around until the Lieutenant found one at the base of a staircase. As he picked it up he looked up at the stairs. The middle part of them seemed to be sagging. He pushed against one of the upright supports that was still standing. It gave way. He stepped back quickly as the entire staircase collapsed and crashed onto the ground floor.

"Steady on old chap!" exclaimed the Commander as a cloud of dust settled over his uniform.

Jack took the lantern, lit it and lowered himself into the hole. He dropped about six feet. Marmaduke followed him down.

They found themselves in a small stone chamber about six feet square. Jack swung the lantern around and the light revealed a small cupboard inset into one of the walls. It was locked.

Marmaduke pulled a dagger out of his belt and inserted it behind the lock. He gave a tug and the lock became lose. He tugged again and again. Finally, the lock broke and the door fell open. Jack lifted the lantern up and they looked inside the cupboard. Inside were a number of tightly wrapped, waterproof packages, There were also two large leather bound ledgers and a number of loose sheets of paper.

Jack reached up and took the top sheet. He held it up in the light of the lantern. He scanned a few lines and then looked up at Marmaduke.

"It's written in Dutch!" he said.

Marmaduke shrugged.

A voice shouted down the hole. It belonged to the Commander.

"Are you alright down there?" he asked.

Marmaduke looked up to see three anxious faces looking down on him.

"More opium. I'll start passing it up to you." He answered.

As he passed the packages up Jack continued leafing through the papers, then he opened one of the ledgers and started thumbing through the pages. He looked up at Marmaduke with a smile on his face.

"It's their ledger. Every shipment that passed through here for the last two years." A frown crossed his face. "The only thing is the figures are all there, but the names and words seem to be in some sort of code."

Marmaduke said nothing but continued passing up the packages. When the cupboard was empty he was about to climb back out of the hole when he looked back into the cupboard. Without saying anything he took out his dagger once again and inserted it into a small crack at the bottom of the cupboard. He gave a quick jerk and a wooden slat sprang up. He reached inside and pulled the slat free, revealing a secret compartment. Jack lifted the lantern up once again. Inside the recess were more papers and a small black book. He slid them inside his jacket and after making sure the compartment was empty he nodded at Marmaduke.

"I think that's everything!" he said.

The pair of them clambered out of the hole and back inside the ruined building.

Jack climbed over the rubble and left the building. Outside he walked towards his horse and very carefully placed the black book, ledgers and loose papers into his saddlebag. He turned around to see where Agnes was treating one of the wounded troopers. She looked up and gave him a wink.

"Got everything?" She asked.

Jack nodded. "I think so!"

Agnes lifted her hand and twitched her finger. The saddlebag glowed slightly and then returned to normal.

"It's safe now!" She said.

Jack gave her a look. "What is it?" he asked.

Agnes shrugged "That's for the Colonel-with-no-name to find out. We've done our bit!"

She turned around and helped the injured trooper onto the rear of the cart placing him carefully among his wounded comrades.

It was a strange procession that led over the moorland road. A troop of soldiers led by the Garrison Commander and his Lieutenant followed by a long straggling line of prisoners stumbling and shuffling along between two rows of mounted troopers. Behind then were two carts. One carried the wounded, the other carried the illicit opium and the chest containing the army payroll. At the side of the chest were the still sleeping forms of the Dutch spies. Sitting up, next to the driver was a very bruised and battered O'Flynn.

Four riders trotted behind the carts. To all eyes, they appeared to be three highwaymen accompanied by an elderly lady who seemed to be riding a horse far too big for her. The sight caused a deal of head scratching for all who saw it.

Chapter Thirteen

The next few days saw a lot of comings and goings at the Garrison inside Scarborough Castle. As soon as the party had arrived the cart with the army gold and opium had been placed under lock and key in one of the strong rooms deep inside the Castle's ancient keep. A dozen armed troopers were ordered onto a twenty-four-hour guard with strict instructions to shoot first and ask questions later.

O'Flynn along with the other injured troopers had been treated in the Garrisons sick bay. Some, the more seriously wounded, were still there.

Unheralded and unannounced the Colonel-with-no-name had arrived and, along with Agnes, Marmaduke, Jack and Mary, returned to the boarding house in Robin Hood's Bay where, to the great curiosity of the locals, had cordoned off the building and searched it from top to bottom. Floors had been ripped up, wooden panelling torn down, secret hiding places and passageways had been discovered and explored. In the kitchen Agnes sat at the table looking into her scrying bowl, searching for and discovering new possible hiding places.

Outside the building, the Colonel-with-no-name stood by the door looking across the square and the slipway. Jack and Mary stood by his side. They watched as the local labourers put the finishing touches to repairing the damaged stonework. The Colonel turned to Jack.

"Your handiwork?" he asked.

Jack nodded.

The Colonel looked thoughtful. "O'Flynn, do you think we can trust him?"

Jack said nothing but continued looking at the repaired slipway. The Colonel followed his look.

"It was over there where the body of the Dutchman was found wasn't it?" The Colonel asked.

Jack looked at him. The Colonel looked back.

"I do read the reports!" he grunted and turned back to look across the Bay.

He continued. "The question is, if you hadn't made contact with him would he ever have reported in?"

Jack shrugged. "Who knows? Although up on the moor I did invite him to join his men before the shooting started."

The Colonel-with-no-name looked back at Jack. "And how far would he have got before either you or Mary shot him?"

Jack thought for a few seconds. "About ten yards!" He paused and then added, "But Mary might have been quicker!"

They turned around and made their way back into what remained of the boarding house. As they entered the kitchen Agnes looked up from her bowl.

"I think that's everything!" She remarked.

They looked through to the hallway where a small chest was guarded by half a dozen troopers.

"More opium!" Marmaduke remarked brushing some dirt from the front of his jacket.

"But you're probably more interested in these." He reached inside his jacket and pulled out a small ledger and some lose papers and dropped them onto the table.

The Colonel-with-no-name picked up the ledger and flicked through its pages. He put it down again and began looking through the papers. Then he looked at Marmaduke and Agnes.

"Everything is in Dutch, and it's in code!" He said.

His disappointment was obvious. He placed the papers back on the table and gave a shrug.

"We can translate it, but it won't make any sense, dammit!"

Agnes looked across at Jack. "Could you bring in your saddlebag please?" She asked.

Jack shook his head. "I didn't bring it with me. Different horse. It'll be back in the stables at the Castle."

Agnes gave a little tut and repeated the question. This time she gave Jack one of those looks.

"Saddlebag?" She asked.

Jack said nothing but turned and left the kitchen. No one said anything until he returned. He was holding his saddlebag. There was a puzzled expression on hs face as he placed in on the table. Agnes moved her fingers and the leather glowed slightly then returned to normal.

"Would you be so kind as to look inside Colonel!" She asked.

The Colonel-with-no-name said nothing but opened the pouch and extracted a small leather-bound ledger. It was the one they had found at Saltersgate. The Colonel opened it up and examined a page. Then he turned the page and examined the next, and the next. Then he sat down and read some more. Then he looked up.

"It's a cipher!" he said.

Agnes smiled. "Fancy that!" she said.

The Colonel didn't hear. He had returned his attention to the book. Eventually, he put it down once again and looked up at Agnes.

"Have you any idea whatsoever what this is? He asked as he tapped the book with hs fingers.

Agnes looked back at him."Let me hazard a guess," She said, then closed her eyes. "It's the book you need to break the Dutch ciphers. Using that you will be able to discover details of whatever's left of their spy network. Not only that but if you examine some of those papers they will reveal the Dutch shipping movements out in the North Sea. It will give you the details of their boat and how it is protected by the Dutch fleet. I think they will reveal or confirm your suspicions that the opium and the spy network originated high up in the Dutch government."

She paused and waited for the Colonel to say something. He didn't, he was too busy reading through the book again.

Two days later a group of people were assembled in the office of the Garrison Commander. It was time for the Colonel-with-no-name and his troops to depart and the Commander always believed in sending his guests off with a hearty breakfast. The group sat around a table heaving with plates of hot loaves, sizzling sausages, slices of bacon, chops, eggs fried, scrambled, poached and boiled. Urns of tea and coffee, and especially for Marmaduke, a large tureen full of kedgeree.

Lieutenant Smalls sat chatting with Mary, showing her the scar the musket ball had made along his neck. Marmaduke sat deep in conversation with Jack. The two army officers were chatting about their exploits in the ongoing American Wars and other skirmishes they had served in. Agnes was in conversation with Andrew Marks and a heavily bandaged O'Flynn who ate sparsely and carefully.

When the meal was over the Colonel-with-no-name rose from the table, Mary, Jack and O'Flynn rose with him. Hands were shaken, promises made, shoulders slapped, and farewells said.

Agnes and Marmaduke, together with the Commander and his Lieutenant stood by the gatehouse as the party left the Castle. It was an impressive sight. Two dozen mounted troopers trotting beside and behind two rather fine carriages that had been acquired. Inside the first carriage were the two Dutch prisoners both wide awake and heavily guarded. They racked their brains as to how they had woken up in such a situation.

In the second coach sat O'Flynn together with, Jack, and Mary. Agnes smiled as she noticed that the two were holding hands. Behind the two carriages was a large heavily guarded cart carrying the opium and the returned army payroll. That was followed by more troopers. As they passed through the gates Agnes gave a little wave. Marmaduke noticed her fingers were moving. Later as they sat in their own kitchen he asked about the moving fingers.

"Nothing much!" she said. "Just a little forgetful spell. They'll remember most of the details, but some things will seem a bit hazy."

Marmaduke raised an eyebrow. "You mean they'll forget about Agnes and her magic?"

Ages placed two of My Tetley's finest tea bags into cups and, as if by magic, they turned into two perfect cups of tea. She handed one to Marmaduke.

"I've told you before. There is no magic. Only tricks!" She said. They both sipped their tea.

END.

ABOUT THE AUTHOR

Graham Rhodes has over 40 years experience in writing scripts, plays, books, articles, and creative outlines. He has created concepts and scripts for broadcast television, audio-visual presentations, computer games, film & video productions, web sites, audio-tape, interactive laser-disc, CD-ROM, animations, conferences, multi-media presentations and theatres. He has created specialised scripts for major corporate clients such as Coca Cola, British Aerospace, British Rail, The Co-operative Bank, Bass, Yorkshire Water, York City Council, Provident Finance, Yorkshire Forward, among many others. His knowledge of history helped in the creation of heritage based programs seen in museums and visitor centres throughout the country. They include The Merseyside Museum, The Jorvik Viking Centre, The Scottish Museum of Antiquities, & The Bar Convent Museum of Church History.

He has written scripts for two broadcast television documentaries, a Yorkshire Television religious series and a Beatrix Potter Documentary for Chameleon Films and has written three film scripts, The Rebel Buccaneer, William and Harold 1066, and Rescue (A story of the Whitby Lifeboat) all currently looking for an interested party.

His stage plays have performed in small venues and pubs throughout Yorkshire. "Rambling Boy" was staged at Newcastle's Live Theatre in 2003, starring Newcastle musician Martin Stephenson, whilst "Chasing the Hard-Backed, Black Beetle" won the best drama award at the Northern Stage of the All England Theatre Festival and was performed at the Ilkley Literature Festival. Other work has received staged readings at The West Yorkshire Playhouse, been short listed at the Drama Association of Wales, and at the Liverpool Lesbian and Gay Film Festival.

He also wrote dialogue and story lines for THQ,

one of America's biggest games companies, for "X-Beyond the Frontier" and "Yager" both winners of European Game of the Year Awards, and wrote the dialogue for Alan Hanson's Football Game (Codemasters) and many others.

OTHER BOOKS BY GRAHAM A RHODES

"Footprints in the Mud of Time,
The Alternative Story of York"

"More Poems about Sex 'n Drugs & Rock 'n Roll
& Some Other Stuff

"The York Sketch Book." (a book of his drawings)

"The Jazz Detective."

"The Collected Poems 1972 – 2016"

The Agnes the Scarborough Witch Series

"A Witch, Her Cat and a Pirate."

"A Witch, Her Cat and the Ship Wreckers."

"A Witch, Her Cat and the Demon Dogs"

"A Witch, her Cat and a Viking Hoard"

Photographic Books

"A Visual History of York." (Book of photographs)

"Leeds Visible History" (A Book of Photographs)

"Harbourside – Images of Scarborough Harbour" (A book of photographs available via Blurb)

"Lost Bicycles" (A book of photographs of deserted and lost bicycles available via Blurb)

"Trains of The North Yorkshire Moors" (A Book of photographs of the engines of the NYMR available via Blurb)

Made in the USA
Middletown, DE
01 April 2017